The Exit Coach

A novella and stories

Also by Megan Staffel

The Exit Coach

A novella and stories
Megan Staffel

Four Way Books
Tribeca

For Graham, Arley, Annabeth

Please direct all inquiries to:
Editorial Office
Four Way Books
POB 535, Village Station
New York, NY 10014
www.fourwaybooks.com

This is a work of fiction. Names and characters, places, events, and businesses are the product of the
author's imagination or are used fictitiously.

Library of Congress Cataloging-in-Publication Data

Names: Staffel, Megan, 1952- author.
Title: The exit coach : a novella and stories / by Megan Staffel.
Description: New York, NY : Four Way Books, [2016]
Identifiers: LCCN 2016007110 | ISBN 9781935536802 (softcover : acid-free paper)
Classification: LCC PS3569.T16 A6 2016 | DDC 813/.54--dc23
LC record available at http://lccn.loc.gov/2016007110

This book is manufactured in the United States of America and printed on acid-free paper.

Four Way Books is a not-for-profit literary press. We are grateful for the assistance
we receive from individual donors, public arts agencies, and private foundations.

This publication is made possible with public funds from the New York State Council on the Arts,
a state agency.

[clmp]

We are a proud member of the Community of Literary Magazines and Presses.

Distributed by University Press of New England
One Court Street, Lebanon, NH 03766

Contents

"As long as I know that you understand," he whispered. "But of course you do. It's a great satisfaction to have got somebody to understand. You seem to have been there on purpose."

"The Secret Sharer," Joseph Conrad

Leaving The Meadows

Two people came through the double glass doors of a twelve-story brick building and walked along the chain link fence to the parking lot. The tall, gray-haired man guided the short, white-haired woman by her elbow, urging her into a more energetic pace. Their heads were canted forward at the same watchful thrust, and anyone looking at them would have guessed correctly they were mother and son. The man was a solid six feet, not fat, but bullish in the shoulders and chest, and the woman, probably tall when she was younger, was now stooped and hollowed. The son's tailored suit and expensive, well-made shoes reported success in the world, and his impatient pace, while the never-slowing lanes of traffic whizzed by the fence, suggested deadlines and engagements. Poor men stop to look at their environment; wealthy men pass through it on their way to somewhere else.

Though the old woman no longer had the same large body as her son, her face still had the vigor of opposition, evident in the stubborn, demanding chin. Leaning on her cane, hobbling beside him, she argued loudly, "I told you we can't go yet. I didn't say goodbye to my friend."

He didn't slow down, but he turned his head to say, "Gloria?"

"I have to say goodbye to her. She won't know where I've gone."

"You've said goodbye to her five or six times already. All right? Okay? You're done with saying goodbye to Gloria."

She stopped, "I'm not done," but the man kept going. "And what if I don't like this new place?" she shouted.

He had reached the car. "What's there not to like? It's very nice." (He had never actually seen it.) "They have animals. It's in the country."

Now she reached the car too. "But the people. Are they friendly?"

"Very friendly."

"What are they like?"

"They're like you. They're old."

"But I have to be back at five thirty. For dinner."

"No, we're leaving. Remember? This is your last day in Buffalo, your last day at The Meadows. And god help me, here's your final goodbye."

He forced her around to get a last look at the enormous structure on one of the city's busiest highways. The Meadows was a brick building built in the seventies that blighted the entire block with its tall, institutional façade and apron of black parking lots. "Goodbye Meadows," he said, as though to a child, not bothering to hide his exasperation.

"Goodbye Meadows," she repeated in a pure, obedient tone.

Sylvia Fleming hadn't been in a car in many years. Within the fortress, a resident's every need had been taken care of, and the few times it had been necessary to venture into the outside world, The Meadows provided a van which picked up and delivered residents to the garage in the basement so their feet never touched the earth and their lungs never breathed anything but interior air. Like many other people who lived there, Sylvia hadn't worn anything but slippers since the day she entered. She didn't own a pair of shoes anymore and earlier that morning, John's brief glance at her flaking, bluish feet with their thick, raptor-like toenails had been enough to dissuade him from any attempt to take her to a store and purchase more ground-appropriate footwear.

Once they got on the interstate, he waited for her to fall asleep, but she stayed awake the entire time, making conversation.

"How's Mary?"

"I don't know, Mom. Mary moved to California. She and I are separated. A year ago, remember?"

"Right. I'm so mixed up I don't know if I'm coming or going. By the way, no one asked me if I wanted to move."

"Look, for the last time: You can't stay there any longer. The Meadows has already rented your apartment to someone else."

"Who told them they could do that? I happen to live there."

"You did live there and now you're moving away."

"Really."

He could see her staring at the complicated structure of bridges and ramps, the pillars that held up the massive swaths of concrete that loomed over the flat, industrial landscape of western New York, moving millions of cars in an infinite combination of directions. "It cost a lot, didn't it? I was running out of money."

"You're right. This new place is cheaper. By half."

"How's your friend?"

"What friend?'"

"Your friend from work who came with you once."

"Bentley? That was a long time ago. But actually, he's the one who discovered this new place. It's called Flora and Fauna."

"That's nice. Like The Meadows."

"Not really. This place is out in the country. It's much smaller. They have a garden and chickens and I think the food will be better."

"So how's Mary? Why didn't she come with you?"

A month ago, when the report came that Mrs. Fleming's mental and physical deterioration required a greater level of care than The Meadows could offer, they recommended The Orchards, their sister institution where each resident had a room rather than an apartment, and access to nursing and hygiene staff twenty-four hours a day. John had been tempted to say yes. It would have meant The Meadows movers and The Meadows van would have done the relocation and his only job would have been to sign a check. But something had made him pause. He wanted to do right for his mother, a person he had once loved, or at least, looking at the childhood photographs, it appeared he must have. Now he felt a mixture of guilt and duty, so he assigned the matter to Bentley. Two days later, Bentley put him on the phone with a woman named Rose Curtain. She was a registered nurse and she operated a home in the southern tier of New York State that provided just the level of care his mother needed. When he asked about vacancies, Ms. Curtain had said, "We're not a large place. We never have more than three, and last week, well, our dear ninety-eight-year-old Arnie climbed the hill and his beautiful, south facing room is available."

"Arnie climbed the hill?"

The Meadows had phoned again and requested that Mrs. Fleming be removed by the end of the month. "Deteriorating hygiene," the officious caller informed him, "is the first sign the resident needs more extensive oversight. And the reports show that Mrs. Fleming..." But seeing Bentley step into his office, John ended the phone call. "So who is Rose Curtain?"

His employee stopped in the center of the room. "Rose? Well, very reliable. Very dependable. You would be satisfied, and I think your mother would be happy."

"But who is she? How do you know about her place?"

Before answering, Bentley looked at the carpet. Then he looked up, and if John had hoped to see anything but the usual expression, he was disappointed. Bentley was never combative, nor arrogant, nor even mildly self-assured. His manner was apologetic, as though by his mere presence he might intrude. If John were given to wondering, which he wasn't, he might have wondered if the many hours Bentley sat at his desk absorbing the shadowless blue of the computer screen had sucked all that was robust out of his body. His skin was the color and texture of eggshell. His hair was never anything but unwashed, and the mole on his neck sprouted a whisker. Though he had solid brown eyes, they were so unquestioning as to be without depth. Bentley was a quiet sufferer, just as he was a quiet accomplisher, and he had, over the years, earned John's admiration. Lucky Cow, the company John had bought as a young man out of business school and grown from a small cheese-making business into a corporation with national distribution and universal name recognition, reflected not only the economic aggressiveness of John Fleming, but the inventive genius of Bentley Tomes.

Bentley knew cows. He knew cheese. That was his world. But when John saw that the business would not grow as he had envisioned unless it had broader appeal, he had developed a new division. Lucky Cow moved into the processed line and that line grew steadily while the line of natural products stayed flat. His business sense told him to drop it, and from that point on, he let demand dictate the direction the company took. As it turned out, Bentley, the farm boy, was willing to accept these changes and soon had learned his way around the world of food science. He hired the people who knew how to make a commodity that tasted like cheese, looked like cheese, smelled like cheese, but was made entirely out of soybeans. And now, pressured by the demands of the stockholders, a noisy crowd who had no patience with the volatility of a major ingredient that was dependent on weather and soil and other variables, Bentley had found the people who could create a commodity with the same CRA, *cheese recognition attributes,* but none of the unpredictability of actual food. They were considering inert materials. Still being tested were wood pulp derivatives mixed with coagulants. But could you get the public to eat a food that wasn't a food at all?

It was Bentley who finessed that question. One ounce of Lucky Cow cheese product would satisfy the daily adult requirements of seven essential vitamins and minerals.

"Which ones?" John asked. "Because calcium, these days, is very popular."

There was a mystery at the center of Lucky Cow. Mary had identified it one night in the midst of an argument and her succinct, biting description stayed with him long after she had left. *Why do I think you don't care? Because the guy you put all of your trust in, the guy you depend on, you haven't even bothered to get to know. I know him better than you do. Because you're incurious. People don't interest you, John Fleming, only things. Accumulated things.*

Some of that was not true. They had worked together thirty years, and John actually did know something about Bentley. He was not married. He did not have a girlfriend. Two facts. Both were understandable, given his behavior. Bentley was not a sexual being. There: a third fact. And yet, he was always sympathetic to John's ongoing problems with Mary and his children and the various women he'd been involved with since she left. Maybe he was willing to listen because he didn't have a personal life of his own. Maybe he was a closet something or other. If so, matter closed. John did not need to know any more about it, but now, watching him figure out how to answer the question about Rose, it came to him that perhaps Bentley was simply a virgin.

He stayed at his spot in the middle of the carpet, hands in his pockets. "We went to school together. My family's dairy farm was next to her family's dairy farm. Now she raises heifers."

"She was your girlfriend?"

John saw a blush fill his employee's cheeks even as he glanced down at his shoes, and then, sheepishly, back up at John. Bentley was wearing the same tan pants and tan jacket he always wore and the redness of his face with the worn and stained outfit made him appear even more scrappy. Several years ago, John had tucked a hefty Christmas bonus into a card with a note, *Go treat yourself*. He'd scribbled the name of "his man" at the only decent gentleman's clothiers in Erie, where the corporate headquarters of Lucky Cow, because of financial advantages in the state of Pennsylvania, had relocated eleven years ago. But it didn't change. The same perma-press jacket and slacks.

"In high school," Bentley said. "But her father surprised us in the hayloft and she was sent away to a boarding school."

"How awful," John said, seeing everything a little too clearly. Bentley, in his awkward, forthright manner, attempting to ravage the girl next door, while all the little rustles and squeals that come with private acts alerting the murderous father. The pulling out, the terror, the slinking away. It would have wounded him for life.

Or maybe there hadn't even been the chance for fucking. That was worse. To be surprised just when they were working up to it, to have the farmer stop it so violently that the shrunken, guilty prick stayed shrunken and guilty forever. Either way it was sad.

"On your recommendation we'll check it out. I'll pick my mother up on Saturday." But that was a lie. There was no time to check it out; he'd have to move his mother right in, unless, of course, the place simply wasn't safe. "Any of your family still in the area?"

"All gone." Bentley's voice was without emotion, his skin back to its normal whitish tone. He had no more to say, and so, with characteristic awkwardness, he turned and went out the door. John watched the worn heels of Bentley's shoes, the baggy backside of his trousers pass into the hallway. It occurred to him that the horror of that night in his friend's adolescence might explain everything. But insights of this nature, revealing private things, made John uncomfortable. Automatically, his fingers started to move across the keyboard. Toneless clicks filled the room and hundreds of exquisitely neutral numbers crossed the computer's face.

The road was so empty and the odor of urine rising from his mother's seat so sharp, that his foot had pressed the accelerator to the floor. The black Mercedes shot through the lush, green landscape like a stone fired with a boys sure aim from his slingshot.

The sign for Flora and Fauna was tiny, but he saw it just in time and made the turn. He pulled up in front of a farmhouse flanked by dilapidated outbuildings. Sylvia sat in the car, waiting until John came around to open her door. Then she unbuckled her seatbelt, set her cane on the ground, and very slowly placed one slippered foot next to it. The other followed, whereupon John leaned in and hoisted his mother onto her feet. Real ground. True air. She sniffed it. "I remember this," she said.

They faced the house. The clapboard needed painting; the porch needed repair. There was an old barn and a field next to it with cows.

"What's that?" Sylvia asked when a shrill bird-like sound startled them both.

"I believe it's a chicken, they cackle."

A small, white dog ran towards them, its tail wagging.

"But John, we forgot to get my things."

"No, Mom, everything's been taken care of. The movers came after we left and packed it all up. I've seen to everything."

"No one asked me. Not once. Do you realize that? And I have to go to the bathroom. Fast."

But after three hours, Sylvia's bathroom announcements no longer created the urgency they had at first. "Not a problem. I'm sure someone here can help you." John took his mother's elbow and pulled her across the rough, uneven grass. The screen door was closed, the cool breath of an empty hallway coming through it. He rapped on the doorframe. "Hello?"

"You're here already!" a voice sang from deep in the interior. "Just a second! I'll be right there!"

"I don't have those pads or those disposable..." his mother remarked in a loud voice.

"You're fine." At each of the four rest areas, he'd guided her as far as the door of the Women's and then dutifully waited outside to guide her back. Beyond that, he had no wish for information. "I'm sure she'll have them."

Color splashed across the screen and a woman with a mass of red hair and a wide, unrehearsed smile pushed it open. Bosom leading—she had the imperiousness common to large-chested women, people like his ex-wife—she stepped barefoot onto the porch and clapped her hands together.

"You've arrived, Sylvia Fleming! How very good of you to come on such a beautiful day!" She pulled his mother into her body for a hug. "And John Fleming."

She was about to hug John too, but he stepped away and put out his hand.

"I've seen you before," Sylvia said.

"My name is Rose. I bet you're tired and thirsty. I bet you'd like to see your room."

"What we need, I believe, is a bathroom," John whispered.

"But first, I'll show you the bathroom and help you get settled."

"I've been here before," Sylvia announced as Rose, holding her hand, stopping to slip her feet into a pair of rubber sandals that were waiting inside the door, led his mother down the hallway. She moved at the old woman's pace so patiently there might not have been such a thing as time or other places to get to.

The floors glimmered and on a shelf he saw a vase of garden flowers.

"I know you."

"Yes, you do. I'm Rose."

"I was so rushed I didn't bring any pads or any of those disposable…."

"Don't you worry. I have everything you need. This is the bathroom. Let me show you."

When the door shut behind them, John found himself alone in the hallway, eavesdropping as they chattered comfortably. "Exactly," Rose was saying, "they go back in here. So you'll always know where they are."

"I remember. John brought me to your house before, because I remember that they go in there."

"I'm glad it feels familiar. Then you won't have to be nervous about moving in with us."

"Oh no, I'm not nervous. I know you and I know this place. But The Meadows is where I live and I want to get back there because they're going to wonder where I am." She added in a polite tone, "You've been very kind to let me use your bathroom."

Sylvia came out first and pronounced it a very nice place. "I would come here if I didn't already have an apartment somewhere else."

"Good, let me show you the bedroom."

Rose took them to the end of the hallway and when she opened a door, a blaze of yellow light fell across the floorboards. "It gets the afternoon sun so this is where I keep my plants."

They stepped into a large room filled with greenery. It had a single bed, a reading chair, and an enormous birdcage where a bird of many colors eyed them warily. "Sammy! Sammy!" it shrieked.

His mother hobbled up to it and said, "I'm Sylvia. Can you say Sylvia?"

"That's Maurice. He loves Sammy and he's always hoping that when the door opens it's going to be her."

"You'll have to learn to say Sylvia," his mother chided, clucking at Maurice as though she were familiar with the ways one made friends with parrots. "He knows me. See, we've been roommates before."

The bed was covered with a soft blue quilt. Tiers of houseplants were arranged in front of the windows. It would be like sleeping in a terrarium, John thought.

"Dinner's at five thirty. I really must get back."

"Mom, we've been through this. You're done with The Meadows. They kicked you out."

"What do you mean? They didn't kick me out." She straightened herself up and in a queenly tone corrected him: "I am a resident."

"You need more care. And you'll get more care here. And that's final. You have to get it into your head. This is your new place." He couldn't help it. Even though he knew very well that she wasn't being dense on purpose, it had been a long day and all he really wanted was to have everything settled.

"There's Sammy," Rose said, slipping her hand into his mother's. "Can you see her over there? She comes every afternoon to help me."

Rose pointed out the window, and in the distance behind the barn, John saw something moving. But it wasn't a person.

"She's a senior in high school. She lives nearby and it's faster coming over the hill," Rose said.

As they watched, the movement took on definition and though he found it hard to believe at first, he realized as the object approached that it was indeed what it had seemed: a girl with long hair whipping about was galloping towards them on a brown horse.

"I know I've been here before," Sylvia said in a soft and amazed voice. "I've seen that hill. I've seen that rider."

They watched her dismount and lead the horse into the barn.

"Sam does the evening rounds, although right now you're our only resident."

"This room is very pretty," Sylvia said. "I like it. I like the view. There's so much to look at."

John consulted his watch. They'd been there an hour and it was clear that the place would be fine. He clasped his mother's hand and said, "I have to go now," his voice thick with a sorrow that had nothing to do with this leave-taking.

"Drive carefully." She was practiced in the routine of goodbye. She waited for the touch of his lips to her forehead and then made the remembered motherly remarks. "Don't worry about me. And next time, bring Mary."

The lake was only a few miles north of the highway. But there was no evidence of a huge body of water just beyond the hills. Just as well. His mind, empty of the usual "to do" list, watched the beautiful, black machine eat up the miles while his memory snagged itself on a conversation.

You're nothing but a robot, she had said to him in the early hours of the day they had decided to separate. *You don't take anything into consideration except money. Money's the ultimate goal.*

"Go ahead," he'd said sarcastically. "Don't hold back. Now that you're telling me what you really think, why not unburden yourself?"

Okay John. Then what about doing good? What about making a quality product? What about contributing to people's health and well-being? Well, why go on. I won't waste my breath.

He remembered how beautiful she had appeared at that moment, how wise and womanly and sad. But she couldn't blame him for economics. "Numbers don't lie. And I'm a good businessman because I understand growth. For your information, growth is necessary for a healthy business." He'd finished with the brand of humility he'd learned at the therapist's. "I'm good at growth. I'm not good at other things."

That was not entirely true. As he knew all too well, growth was aggression. There were businesses that could plateau and still have healthy balance sheets, but he was too ambitious for that. He'd re-invented the entire cheese landscape and now Lucky Cow was not just a company any longer, but a force. Each time he altered the product it received national attention without even a full-scale advertising campaign and instead of TMS, *targeted market saturation*, they had BMS, *bulk saturation*. Now BMS drove the corporation. Lucky Cow altered packaging or ingredients continuously, simply to gain attention.

The therapist suggested that he and Mary spend a Saturday together every month and for awhile, it seemed to be working. On a Saturday in June, Mary had wanted to explore the lake. They'd found a hidden path that took them to a small cove with a protected beach. The water was cold, invigorating. "Isn't it wonderful?" she cried, dancing about with the simple pleasure of nakedness. He splashed out quickly; it was too cold. But he found a rock to sit on, and watched her play in the water while he rubbed himself dry with his shirt. When she came out, rinsed and glistening, they had moved in concert. He caught a stink of something on the wind, but it was from another cove, so he put it out of his mind, and together, following the lead of their bodies, they dropped down to the sand. But then he felt insects biting his legs, tiny pinpricks of pain, over and over. Sand fleas. He slapped them away until she took his hand and murmured softly, holding his hand to her mouth, her breast, stroking him, kissing him, opening herself. But it started again and finally, he couldn't stand it, he jumped up.

Yes, it was too abrupt, but he couldn't help it, they were annoying him.

Back in the car, Mary's eyes were wet. She was pressed against the door, as far away from him as possible. He couldn't think of the right thing to say, so he nosed the car along the curve of the lake and let it find the one lane blacktop, so unused there were weeds along the edge. It took them to a cove they had never visited. They discovered a hotel that seemed to operate mostly as a restaurant. The elegant, old-fashioned structure was three stories high, with a gingerbread porch cantilevered over the rocks. The tables were filled, the diners dressed as though for a party, women sparkling with jewelry and perfume, white-coated waiters balancing platters heaped with some kind of fish. They found a table on the outer edge, and in the spirit of the party they ordered it too. Smelt. The breaded, crispy, tiny fish, heaped on a silver platter, came with a dipping sauce. Mary was famished. She looked errant, disturbed, laughing too loudly, eating the fish with her fingers, dozens disappearing at once. He nibbled carefully, preferring the beer and celery to creatures that had been dragged from the oily bottom of a polluted lake.

Yes, he knew exactly what his mistakes were. Hadn't they talked about it endlessly? But no amount of hushed dinner-time talk, her greasy fingers lifting the fish to her mouth, her laughter hanging on a precipice where it might at any moment dissolve into tears, could alter the fact that an army of small, stinging insects had attacked his legs and not hers. What was he supposed to do? He said he was sorry but apparently his timing was off. The time for sorry had been earlier. Well he didn't understand then and he didn't understand now how an intelligent adult woman could be so undone by such a tiny thing. Fleas! It was their last outing.

The phone rang. "How'd it go?" the familiar voice asked.

John was tempted to hedge a bit just out of habit. But why? Bentley was his friend. "It's a nice place. I think she'll get good care."

"Great." Bentley paused, taking a moment before revealing the real reason for the call. "What did you think of Rose?"

"Rose is remarkable. She's everything you said. It'll be a nice change from The Meadows. My God, now I realize what a horror that place was."

"Do you think…" but Bentley hesitated and John could see him casting his eyes downwards. "Well, would it be all right, John, if I go there once to visit your mother? Do you think she'll remember me?"

"Absolutely. She'll be happy to see you. I guarantee it."

"Good. I think I'd like to do that. It would give me a chance to say hello to Rose."

"I'm getting into traffic," John said, understanding as soon as the opportunity had passed that he should have suggested they go there together.

But Bentley, who was used to non-engagement, simply went on. "Okay, just listen. The tests are done. We know what to use. It's not straw dust; it's not wood pulp. Too much texture. Get this. It's water. Plain, ordinary water. With seven essential vitamins and minerals, plus the oils and coagulants and stabilizers and flavorings. You know, the list."

Water, John thought, coming into the city, weaving the Mercedes through the ribbons of traffic and then braking suddenly when the line slowed. On a beautiful summer day when he'd seen a girl galloping her horse down a hill, water, that plain and forthright, almost spiritual substance, seemed exactly right.

Tertium Quid

Meredith had entered the age of entropy, and the great media machine of American culture gunned past her, its probes searching out juveniles. Movies, music, TV shows, like bathing suits and bras, were not created for a person like her. Sixty and beyond, it was the age no one wanted to be reminded of, except of course the other women who had reached it also. They were an army that is no longer needed yet still wanders the countryside.

Why wasn't it a celebration? Birth control, pregnancy scares: relics from a bygone era! Nipples, once so eager, poking through the blouse at the cry of an infant, any infant—they were no longer on call! No more blood, no more babies, no more milk! No guilt for staying home with sick children. No sick children fending for themselves while mommy worked. The whole megillah, come to an end, and now a different mixture of hormones that required a tweezers to the chin every once in awhile, extracting the male whisker. What was going to happen next?

She was lucky. She had a husband, also aged, and the two of them had Dr. Zoot. Dr. Zoot was the only one at the frontier who welcomed the troops. Women in their waning years: he liked them.

"Yes indeedy," Dr. Zoot murmured, perched high on a limb of a tree, licking his chops as he watched the troops clanking across the field with their heavy, outdated equipment.

Gregory, the husband, was a few years older than Meredith, but he had a head of hair that was still just as thick and deeply black as it had been when he was young. At least his hairline had receded, but the higher forehead, instead of aging him, conferred wisdom and authority. Tomorrow they were going to the Dexlers for a dinner party, but tonight, why, there was nothing on the calendar. "Hey," Meredith said, draping her arm over Gregory's shoulder, fitting her palm on his nice plump bottom. "Wanna mess around?"

"I'm tired," he said. "I'm going to bed."

"How about I come up and we see what happens?"

Forget it. A thought not voiced. The husband had been trained. "I'd really look forward to doing that with you some time, but tonight I'm really tired. I have to get horizontal. My back aches."

"You're sure? I can't do a little convincing? Maybe the doctor is interested."

"The doctor is not interested."

"How do you know? Sometimes he surprises us."

"Not this time. Trust me, nothing's going to happen."

Dr. Zoot had grown older too, but he hadn't noticed. It seemed the male ego was indestructible, while the female ego, those sad, tired soldiers marching through the hot, deserted fields, grew dispirited. Of course, Dr. Zoot was not the actual phallus. He was chief of staff, spokesperson. The phallus itself . . . well, it was one of the mysteries. Beyond reason, definition, understanding, its inscrutability was perhaps what she liked the most.

Women were certainly more predictable, and, as far as Dr. Zoot was concerned, the naughtier the better. He whirled, he danced, he imagined. In the mornings he peed off the porch in full view of the road and wandered around without trousers, his air-cooled parts still pink and bouncy though some of those hairs were gray.

In reality—but what was that? And whose? Meredith's sophomore year roommate, an aspiring fashion designer named Carmen, had created Dr. Zoot in her sketchbook and he'd become the model for her line of gangster-era clothing.

She'd given him a sinister look. She'd posed him against crime-scene backdrops: on bridges, at loading docks, in railroad yards. "I have to tell you something, Merry. It's about that guy you brought back here. Gregory? Because I'm really a little worried. You probably don't see it, but when I look at him . . . well, it's obvious that it's on his mind every second. Those lips. That line of intense red under the mustache. He wants things. All the time. Do you like it, being his victim?" Poised on small feet that supported, perfectly, her wide, generous frame, Carmen had raised her thin, starved eyebrows. It was 1973, the age of the free and undisciplined body, and not many women plucked.

"No," Meredith replied in a timid voice, even though she knew *no* wasn't the right answer because victim wasn't the right way to describe the thing she had with Gregory. But *yes* wouldn't have worked either.

"Be careful, Meredith. You are not his toy, remember that. You are not a thing for him to play with."

"Right," she replied. "But I'm not. It's not like that. Not at all. It's . . ." She hesitated, realizing suddenly how different they were, looking for a quality Carmen might respect. "Fun." That word was followed by a cold silence. "Cool," Carmen said from her side of the room, then added in a kinder voice, "I just don't want you to be used by him. But if it's fun, then okay. You would know, right?"

Dr. Zoot was a thin man with long hair and a mustache. He walked through the sketchbook in the seven outfits Carmen called the Italian collection. Meredith noticed there was something familiar about the lightly penciled face. Then she realized. It was Gregory wearing the long topcoat, the pleated pants. In one of the drawings he was on the Brooklyn bridge, a machine gun pointed at the Manhattan skyline.

Was she a toy? But she liked it. It was secret and exciting and dark and it was never the same. And if she was a toy, wasn't Gregory one too? It was all so hard to figure out. There were feelings and then there were ideas. And under it all, there was this shared instinct, this thing they'd discovered together, an amazing, breathless ability to explode themselves into new people. Was it only sex? She didn't know. But what was hers or his and who was being used . . . that was old stuff, no longer relevant.

Five years later, they were living together, and one day, apropos of nothing, Meredith said, "Remember my roommate?"

"The one with the big tits. From Queens."

"That's exactly what she would expect you to say. Why the focus on her breasts?"

"They were really big. I was hoping to catch her with her shirt off. Because she always covered them up with all this stuff, I don't know, sweaters or overalls or something."

"That was exactly her point. There you are, thinking about sex, always sex."

"So, what's wrong with that?" There was a completely unperturbed look on Gregory's face. He had short, neatly trimmed hair because the age of the free and undisciplined body was slowly giving way to the age of the super-groomed. Even Gregory. Not only did he cut his hair, he shaved, and when he smiled, she saw the solid clean sweep of his naked jaw.

Gregory taught pottery in an after-school program; Meredith taught acting. She also wrote plays, applied for grants, and did whatever she could to nourish the necessary belief in things that didn't actually exist, like funding and audiences willing to support the dramatic arts. She'd learned to trust the dubious, the hopeful, the almost. Which was why it was necessary to pay attention to the concrete things of her life. Like Gregory's smooth cheekbone. She could lose herself there.

"Dr. Zoot. That's what she called you."

He gave her an uncomprehending look.

"You know, the gangster type. That's what she thought you were. A fornicator, a dirty jokes man, a tits and ass guy."

"But I am," Gregory replied, his beautiful lips stretching wide and the honest slope of his chin melting her insides.

After that, Meredith brought the gangster into their lives. "Sit on that seat!" he cried from the back of their car when they passed a woman in tight nylon shorts cycling down the road. They were used to it. And now, long married, the kids grown up, there was no need to hide. Meredith loved that guy. Who else paid any attention? Who else, in the later years, was still desperate with desire?

When it was just them, in the car or in the house, she would feel a kind of wrinkling in the air and then she'd see his bright blue face, his warty nose and bloodshot eyes. She'd smell cigar smoke, and soon after, she'd hear a remark. "Take it off!" he shouted at a female newscaster who looked worn out and brittle, despite the dyed hair, the youthful clothes, the makeup. Zoot wants you, Meredith could say. But she didn't talk to TVs like he did.

The Dexlers lived on the ridge over the next valley with their two-year-old granddaughter, a Chinese orphan their daughter had adopted and then abandoned when her husband had a nervous breakdown. "It's so sad. Isn't it sad?"

Gregory, from long habit, could guess the context. "I don't know. What else would they be doing?"

"At their age to have to be parents again. To go through it all again. It must be exhausting."

"It could happen to us too. You never know."

"I hope not."

"Well, don't worry, at the rate our guys are going, we won't have any grandchildren at all."

He pronounced it with a finality that surprised her.

"Wouldn't that disappoint you?"

"I don't know, haven't really given it any thought."

"Oh gosh, it would me. I think it would be wonderful." She gushed like any sixty year old considering progeny.

"You can't predict. Who knows? Nothing happens the way you imagine."

Gregory believed in the body. He felt that all things would work out, and though he didn't condone Dr. Zoot's gin and mafia values, he also didn't share Meredith's earth-mother worries. The planet would heal. The species would survive. He'd moved from the body of clay to the human body, and now he was a chiropractor with a small, rural practice.

The car radio, tuned to the local NPR station, whispered the news, and then suddenly a dreadfully loud and cheerful voice sang out from the dashboard, announcing women's career day at the local college. "All area high school girls are invited to visit the Alfred State campus and discover their many options. You can be an accountant, an architectural engineer, a business administrator, a computer programmer, a court reporter . . ."

"A cock sucker!" Zoot shouted from the back seat.

"Imagine a career in the culinary arts, digital animation, forensic science technology . . ."

"Loaded with benefits!" he cackled.

Meredith saw the runny, bloodshot eyes, the moldering, tattered suit. Carmen, wherever she was, would be appalled.

The Dexler compound was a group of buildings situated at the end of a long, freshly graveled driveway. As their car crunched towards it, thick white dust swirled about their windows. Meredith didn't bother to knock because she could hear voices in the back. During the summer, all activities happened outside, behind the house, where there was a generous flagstone patio with a grill, picnic table, and dramatic views plunging in all directions. A huge striped umbrella was opened over the table and, as Meredith helped Sharon carry out drinks and hors d'oeuvres, a catbird performed from the bushes, speaking in the voices of all of the other birds of the neighborhood, trilling and yanking and squeaking at a rapid, insistent volume. By the time dinner was served, the bird had flown and the trees were swathed in darkness. Invisible cicadas, looking for mates, roared into the night.

"We are so lucky," Sharon said. "This paradise. This August music. Honey, did you check her diaper?"

Vern stood up. With his tongs, he set an ear of corn on everyone's plate. "It's fine. And if it's not fine, it can wait. Let's enjoy and not think about it. Besides, she's happy. Look at her."

Everyone turned to the two-year-old sitting in a highchair at the end of the table. Her eyelids fluttered in her flat, peaceful face. There wasn't any food on her plate, but her head was canted backwards, a sippy cup raised to her mouth.

"Very good, Dexlers. Training her to be an alcoholic."

Sharon smiled at Gregory indulgently. "I know. But she refuses to eat anything solid and she loves her sippy cup. I make her drinks in the blender. That way I'm sure she's getting some nourishment."

"So important," Meredith agreed, seeing the land tumble down under the clouds, a sliver of moon rising. There were candles, platters of good things to eat, a bottle of chilled wine. Next to her, the child with the wide face gazed at the sky through secretive eyes. The liquid going into her mouth was purple.

"So what is it?" Meredith asked.

"Well, it's a blend. Whatever I have. Right now, it's tofu, peanut butter, blueberries, spinach, yeast, and soymilk. She likes it. Don't you, Naomi? You like your drink, don't you?"

Hearing her name, the little girl put down her cup and looked at her grandmother.

"Naomi, can you say drink?"

"Dink."

"Listen. Drrrr . . . . . ink."

"Ddd . . . . . ink."

"Good girl! And what is this?" Phyllis picked up an ear of corn.

Naomi put the sippy cup to her mouth and tilted her head back.

"Naomi, what is this?"

She stopped drinking and said, "coin."

"And what is this? Naomi over here, what is this?" Phyllis pointed to her elbow. "You learned this word today, remember?"

Naomi's eyes lowered to her grandmother. "Bow," she said.

"El . . . bow," Phyllis corrected. "Ellllllbow."

Naomi returned to her cup.

"You know why she drinks her meals instead of eating them? It gives her a break from the constant vocabulary test. It's really intense. Did we do that with our kids?"

They were driving home, their headlights pulling them through the dark, humming world. Just as they started the descent from the Dexlers' hill, rain slanted across the road.

Gregory turned on the wipers. "I don't think we did. Plus, it wasn't like that then. There wasn't that constant pressure. Kids could just be kids. They could learn at their own rate. And, remember, our kids weren't Chinese."

"They weren't?"

"They were aliens, but not from China."

In the valley, the rain was steady. "Shit," Meredith said.

"What's the problem?"

"Frogs. See them?"

Strings of fog hung in the twin cones of light and the shapes rising up off the country road might have been leaves blowing in the wind, but the two of them knew from experience that those were frogs. Gregory slowed down. Hundreds were taking advantage of the wet pavement to cross from the marsh on one side of the road to the marsh on the other, and a certain percentage were dying under their tires.

"Can't you steer around them?"

"I'm trying."

There were little frogs and big frogs, low jumpers and high jumpers. They'd flash in the beams for just a second, some going straight across, some going zigzag, some reaching their destination, others not. "I can't stand it."

"Really, Merry, I'm trying. I'm not hitting many at all."

"How do you know? You can't tell. They're disappearing all over the world and this isn't helping. I think you should pull over. I really do."

"Right, and then another car will come along and squash them."

"There are no other cars. No one's on this road at ten thirty at night. Please. Stop."

"It's too late. We have to get home."

"Just pull over and park."

"By the way," Dr. Zoot piped up from the back seat, "rain makes them horny."

"Maybe," Meredith said, ignoring the comment, "she likes the cup because it lets her suck. It's comforting. After all, she's lost two mothers. Maybe Phyllis took her off the bottle too soon." Finally, Gregory was slowing down, moving to the shoulder so the frogs could cross the road without peril. "Thank you," she said.

"Okay, but I just want you to know I have to be at the office at seven in the morning. And look at it. This rain could go on for hours."

"It'll stop soon. I'm sure it will." But really, she knew that they could sit there on the side of the road, eight miles from home, for half the night. The water hit the windshield with that sort of steadiness.

"This kind of weather? They get moist between the legs." The Doctor was standing on the back seat, his oversized face thrust forward towards Gregory's ear.

"I know, I know, but the fact of the matter is that I have to get up really early."

"It must be so confusing," Meredith said. "To feel finished with all of that and then have this tremendous responsibility dumped in your lap. It's huge. It's really huge."

Gregory turned off the motor. "Love gets them through it. Or something. But I'm really tired. And I really need a good night's sleep.

Tomorrow I have a huge day."

"Right. And the frogs too. They need to survive. Just think of all the ones we're saving."

Smoke wafted over their heads and a phlegmy voice said, "She wants it. Look, you did what she asked. Any idiotic thing like that, they're grateful. So, make your move." Zoot waved his cigar in Meredith's direction. "Talk nice. Flatter her up."

"We'll do it tomorrow," Gregory said. "We have to get home. I have to be at the office at six thirty."

"You think she's going to let you go? Trust me. Sit back! Relax! Forget tomorrow! She's ready, I'm telling you. All you gotta do is kissy, kissy, a little tongue action."

The rain drummed the metal rooftop steadily. The smell of wet earth permeated. Dr. Zoot disappeared and it was just the two of them.

Megan Staffel

Mocked and Invaded

When asked, Meredith said she was an actress, and although her resume was a five-page, single-spaced listing of all the roles she'd played over the years in productions across the state, she knew actress didn't describe it. Just as driving, which was what she was doing now, with her husband in the seat beside her, hardly fit the number of activities that made up that moment, only a fraction of which were related to the fact that her right foot pressed the gas pedal and her left foot hovered over the clutch in case she'd have to brake suddenly. Her hands were on the steering wheel and her eyes were sweeping the fields for signs of deer ready to bound out in front of her, but all of that was secondary. Primary was the thinking, remembering, talking, and regretting what she was talking about at the very same time she was uttering the words.

"You were so dazzled by all that glitz and show and just because they have the same kind of approach to medicine that you do, you sort of, I don't know what happens to you." I-messages, she was remembering. Put it in an I-message. "I don't know what happens to you," she said again, hoping that would suffice, and then she went right back to the accusations. "You relax or something. You just lie down and roll over and say yes to everything and you drag me into it and expect me to love them at first sight too and you're totally oblivious to the fact that they're despicable. They had nothing to talk about all weekend except the things they've bought. They're consumers. Yes, they do alternative medicine, but they're consumers first and foremost. Who cares about which kind of fucking bread machine? I hope you were bored," she added.

"Watch it," he said, because a tractor had just pulled onto the little two-lane road ahead of them.

She braked and then downshifted. "I see it." But truthfully, she saw much more than the tractor that was pulling a round bale behind it. She saw the purple hills on either side of the valley, the black road cutting through the impossible green of spring fields that were suddenly naked after a blanket of snow, and the ribbon of mist made by the soft expirations of the newly plowed earth.

They could have taken the interstate, but Meredith liked Route 7, which passed through one small town after another, each with a tattered dignity that was different from the tattered dignity of the town just before it. She wanted to stop and get lunch or a cup of tea but each Main Street they came to was locked down, its store windows empty because customer was a word from the past.

"Were you?" she asked.

"Well, I will admit it wasn't the most thrilling weekend I've ever had, but it was nice to get away and I liked seeing their place and I like them even though . . ."

"They're really superficial," she finished for him.

"We just hadn't found the right things to talk about," he explained in a voice that was patient from the many years of arguments like this one. "And with you slicing them up with your cold blue eyes, no wonder. Just relax. Give them a chance. Babs and Newlander . . . they do really great work, especially with diabetes, which is a huge problem around here." He looked off to the horizon as though up in the low hanging clouds he could see it, diabetes, hanging like a blimp over the land.

"That couldn't be his real name. What mother would name her son Newlander Forbes?"

Gregory didn't hear the sarcasm. "An immigrant mother, one who had great hope for the new land she'd come to, that's who. His mother was from Sicily."

"Even so."

"You're impossible."

"Only because you're so gullible."

She wished they could take Route 7 the whole way home, but the valley was now slowly and imperceptibly tilting them down into the flat plane where the city of Binghamton lay itself out like a drunken idiot and imposed bridges and highways and measureless amounts of concrete onto the riparian meadows of central New York. On the other side of Binghamton there was Elmira. Shopping centers, a tangle of signs. On the other side of Elmira the disastrous weekend at Babs and Newlander Forbes's house came up again, but then they were traveling on the wider, straighter four-lane that so much more quickly brought them over to the western side of the state, and the old sympathies of their long married existence returned.

"It was awful, wasn't it," Gregory said finally. "What a mistake."

And Meredith only kissed his cheek because he was driving and they were on another small road, this one taking them up through the hills to their own much higher valley and he had to be on the lookout for deer.

No, she wasn't really an actress because she didn't live in New York City or Los Angeles and she didn't aspire to anything beyond the regional theater where there had been enough fine moments for her to have a following. But also, there was something else. Some kind of a wall. She wasn't able to pass beyond a certain point. Her times "getting there" came and went; they couldn't be counted on. And in the end they were only the occasional bright spots in a career that included many professional but uninspired performances. She'd never spoken about this to anyone, not even Gregory, because it would sound too bitter, too much like self-pity.

At thirty-one, she'd been an extraordinary Juliet to an adequate Romeo. Her secret was a technique she called mirroring, taking the passion she felt for her husband, back-dating it fifteen years, and directing it towards another man. At thirty-nine she'd been the nurse. Yet as the nurse there wasn't anything to mirror.

'Yea,' quoth he, dost thou fall upon thy face?
Thou wilt fall backward when thou hast more wit;
Wilt thou not Jule and by my holidam,
The pretty wretch left crying and said 'Ay.'

The woman who'd cackled over those lines had subtleties Meredith couldn't reach. So she'd turned her into a buffoon and played for laughs rather than feeling.

At fifty-two she was the wife of Macbeth. That role too was close to her. She took the ordinary desire to tangle in a husband's life and blew it up huge:

Hie thee hither,
That I may pour my spirits in thine ear.

In *The Vagina Monologues*, which she did the same year, she was "The Flood":

Down there? I haven't been down there since 1953.

She was "on" for opening night, but after the reviews and congratulations, the sadness of the story trapped her and she could never again play the woman from the inside. Her empathy was too shallow; it was all used up the first night. And because she herself wasn't a woman like that, and furthermore couldn't imagine the private occasions that had created a woman like that, a certain squeamishness kept her outside the character. Still, she was a professional, so most people didn't notice. But she knew, the director knew, and that's what mattered.

Apart from acting, she was a cook and a gardener. She was also a bird watcher and had, with some success, become a student of bird language. And why not? She knew French already, but was she surrounded by people who spoke it? No. In the small rural outpost where Gregory had his practice, she was surrounded by birds.

Children might have helped. But they'd never gotten around to it. First, theater seasons had intervened and then there were Gregory's loan payments from medical school. So it was the farmhouse that became the object of their mutual attentions. They fixed it up—remodel was a word Meredith would never use for fear of being lumped with people like the awful Forbeses—and now it was functional, though admittedly a bit odd. A large and luxurious bathroom replaced the cramped and ugly original that her character from the *Monologues* would have seen no reason to change.

They put a window over the soaking tub so they could look out on the wetlands, and on spring evenings they bathed and listened to nature's opera, the "come hither" songs of male amphibians.

This evening, the wetlands would be sheeted with ice. The April weather had turned cold, so they carried armloads of firewood into the house along with their jackets and bags.

Home. Its familiar smell, the cat-clawed furniture, the dog-furred rugs. It was not a stylish place. Gregory kneeled at the woodstove in the chilly living room to start a fire, his comfortably pillowed and sweatered middle blocking the delicate structure he was building of paper, kindling, and logs. He held a match to it, and as the flame trembled he pursed his lips like a child at his birthday party and blew. It worked and soon the stove was throwing out heat. The drapes were closed against the night, soup was warming on the stove, and as they sat together and had their dinner, the two days they'd spent in the eastern part of the state were sealed over and forgotten.

But then it started. Wing beats in the wall behind the stove. How could a bird have fallen into a wall? Sometimes a grackle nested in the chimney and when the occasional one tumbled into the living room, flying in panic from rafter to rafter, they'd open the door for him to escape, but how could they rescue a bird in the wall? Hoping it would find a way out, they climbed the stairs to their bedroom. And lying side by side in the old iron bed frame, their heads cradled on familiar pillows, their hands clasped, they entered their separate dreams when suddenly over their heads there was scratching.

"Squirrels," Gregory mumbled. They listened to them running between the joists until finally Gregory—because he was the one to do these things—heaved himself off the mattress, went downstairs, and returned with a broom, which he used to pound the ceiling. It worked. The squirrels got the message. But then, just as sleep was coming on, the sound began again. This time, Meredith turned to her side, draped her leg over her husband's body, threw her arm across his chest, and hanging on as though she were rafting through an ocean of small disturbances, found her way back to the interrupted plot.

At 3:00 a.m. there was a new sound. They both woke up at the same time. In the exterior wall, something with very long teeth and an enormous appetite gnawed through the rigid insulation they'd installed last summer under the siding. "A rat," her husband mumbled. "Everyone's coming in because it got cold."

At 4:45 Meredith gave up. Gregory's breath had the steadiness of slumber, so very carefully she slid from the covers and tiptoed into the next room. When she turned on the light, the windows glared with accusing vacancy. She pulled a blanket around her nightgown and sat down in the upholstered chair.

31

It was 5:00 exactly when the birds began. She heard a song sparrow, a blue jay, a robin. Quietly, she lifted the window. Now she could hear a cardinal. As usual, it was singing loudest of all. But then the dull steady buzz of a chipping sparrow was just as loud. Meredith was puzzled. Both songs came from the same location. And now there was a robin at the very same spot. She counted the number of times the robin's song was repeated and then she knew. Catbirds—but it was too early in the spring for catbirds—repeated songs once, and brown thrashers, the other mimics, repeated them twice. The songs she was hearing now were repeated four and five times, so it was the greatest mimic of them all, the mockingbird. They'd never had a mockingbird in their valley before.

At 5:30 when the light was general, she saw him, a gray bird with a long tail perched at the top of the spruce. Through the binoculars, his profile was distinct in the raw sun of early morning. She crouched below the sill and saw him tilt his head back, open his beak, and issue forth four times another bird's song.

She watched as he imitated the loud commanding towhee and then the small, scolding wren. Each had equal complexity. There was no judgment, no slackening of enthusiasm.

Arrogance

The first year we were married, Richard and I made love in every state between New York and California. We thought our bodies would never wear out. We camped in national parks at night and in the daytime we toured famous gardens. We began with the Sonnenberg, near us in Canandaigua, and ended at the Golden Gate Conservatory. In St. Louis it was the Shaw; we spent two days wandering the eighty acres, coming home at night to Richard's grandfather's apartment.

It's curious, but what I remember from that trip now is not the feat of geographical sex, or the wonders of highly manipulated landscapes, but something the old man told us. We were standing in the narrow hallway of his large and comfortable apartment, looking at a wall of photographs that showed him as a young man, and though he was still just as well-dressed and elegant, age had made him fragile. His body was stooped and starved-looking, but his brain was sound and his eyes were lively. "I can't believe I'm eighty-seven," he whispered. "How did it happen?" At that time the question seemed irrelevant. Richard's grandfather might have succumbed to eighty years, but I knew, at age twenty-three, that I would have the strength and better sense to avoid it.

This was not because I thought I would die young, or because my generally pessimistic view of international affairs accepted the probability of a devastating nuclear event; the fact is, I really did believe I would never be older than thirty-six, the age I had once chosen with a friend as the last outpost before the decrepitude neither of us would ever consent to experience.

The problem, now that I'm well past that outpost and others, meaning that I'm a post-puberty, post-fertility, post-everything woman: how does one go forward? What does the baby-making body do now? I remember the hallway. It was painted a soft canary yellow and the little man was so excited to see us. How did it happen, he asked. He knew and I do too. No one can escape time. For me, the question is still in the present tense: How does it happen?

What I mean, of course, is Hagar. My friend with the unfortunate name. I've never asked her about it. And the truth is, now that we like each other, I never think of her namesake at all. When I think about her, which I do fairly often, it is her youth I think of, her new motherhood. Just now, she called to ask if we had internet, theirs was down, could she come by to get online?

I go outside to wait for her. In October, there are always things to do. Weeds to pull, hoses to bring in, plants to mulch with the straw stored in the barn, so as I wait, I also accomplish things. What I've always told people who come to my gardening clinics is that what you do in the fall, that is, the way you put your gardens to bed for the winter, will, to a large extent, determine the success of your efforts the following spring. Trim, weed, mulch. It's the October mantra, a gardener's way of saying thank you and goodbye to the beds that have given so much food and pleasure. The mulch provides extra housing against the wind that will rage across our hilltop in November and the heavy snows that will follow. October is as busy for me as May, the month the gardens finally wake up from death.

Hagar is not interested in vegetables or flowers. And of course gardening is harder when you have an infant. My children survived it, each established now in a different part of the country, but sometimes I wish I hadn't been so ambitious. I wish I had slowed down and enjoyed their first years rather than stowing them away in the various places I had for stowing them, so I could get on with my business.

That's how I thought of it. The gardens were my means of expression. I knew I shouldn't let them go entirely, but I couldn't even cut back. So every season but winter was frantic.

I don't mention these things to Hagar. What young mother wants someone giving advice? Especially when you're cramming your daughter's first year with important other things. So I don't tell her about my regrets, and instead talk about Richard, far from the internet, tucked away for ten months in a life of research, one of six international biologists mapping the life cycle of the African savannah, the place they believe was the home of humanity's first progenitors. Because Hagar is a new friend, she has never met Richard. But she's seen photographs, she's heard parts of his letters, and she believes that marriages get better when husband and wife spend time apart. "Doing what they have to do," is the way she puts it, giving it the uplifting tone of sacrifice.

I don't confess that loneliness makes me so desperate sometimes I am unable to go into my empty house, that I stay here, outside, all day with the plants. I walk through the rattling leaves of dying corn, past the frost-ruined basil. My eye travels out to the tamaracks in the field. Come November they will turn yellow and the needles will fall to the ground, but by then everyone will be asleep but the evergreens. What will I do? A long winter alone up here on the hill worries me. But that's another thing I haven't mentioned.

I could see Hagar at the end of our lane, just beginning the long, uphill climb, her tires churning the gritty dust on a loose road bed that will be plowed this winter, not by Richard but by Bud, the neighbor between us. I waved once, in case she happened to be looking towards the gladiola circle, and then bent down to continue digging them up.

The car was going fast; I could hear stones hurled against its undersides. Hagar was in a rush. In a flash she was parked, and then Lily was already unbuckled and in her arms, curtained by heaps of unruly brown hair. I embraced it all: hair, woman, child.

Colors do not clash, she once told me, and it's a belief she adheres to. Today she was wearing orange pants and a loose red blouse. Hagar's skin is as smooth and creamy as the petals on the little magnolia I planted in a wind-protected corner of our property and now am mulching heavily because it's really not supposed to survive our climate. Her face has the same slight blush of pink and her eyes light up when she looks at me, though she dispenses with greetings always. There's no hello or smile, no initiating comment about the weather, but a look full of intention, as though we were in the middle of an ongoing conversation. I find it thrilling. Hagar pulled away, thrusting the child towards me—"Hold Lily, will you? I have to get online"—and ran into my house.

I have always felt that when friendship achieves this level of informality it's secure, but ours, I must say, reached it almost immediately because Hagar is a person who assumes the other is perfectly willing to respond to her many requirements. I tucked Lily against my body and chattered to her as we walked among my beds. At four months, she fit my arms perfectly. When she was still. But when she got fidgety, which she was starting to do as she realized that the person who held her lacked the reassuring odor of breast milk, she became awkward. I shifted her to an upright position so I could pat her back and we continued our stroll. As I showed her the leeks and collards that were still growing in the garden, I was talking all the time, telling her how sweet the greens became after frost and that I'd cut some so her mother could cook them for dinner, but she would not be consoled. I tried thumping her back. That often works. The theory is to distract her from hunger by providing her with another sensation that's just as strong. I kissed the sun-warmed top of her head and cupped my hand around her firm little skull. My hand fit her head perfectly and she rode in the chair that my hips made, her arm stretching across my breast for security. I noticed, not for the first time, how well a woman's body is designed for this portage.

My daughters live on the other side of the continent. I see them twice a year. There was a time when Richard and I talked about moving closer, but we couldn't leave our gardens. "Oh Lily," I say, "let me show you the winter squash." I take her into the shed and show her the rows of vegetables and I can feel her respond to the excitement of my voice. "It's called delicata." I point to a funny striped one and she coos.

Hagar found us with the carrots. They were laid out to dry in the garage, and this year they were so big and thick they looked obscene. Hagar saw it too. "Why, Nancy—vegetable dildos?"

Lily is ecstatic. She wiggles up and down and lifts her arms, making the noises that will bring the goddess of milk to our side.

"I know what *you* want." Hagar takes her daughter and walks to the patio where the summer furniture is still set out. She asks for a glass of water, which I bring happily, and then I sit down too. Hagar nurses without prudishness, the rounded white top of her breast exposed so her daughter's hand could grasp it, the hair falling over them both, and the long and interesting messages flashing in the depths of her dark eyes as she talks. My neighbor with the Old Testament name is a fiber artist. That means that though she knits and crochets and weaves things on looms, she makes absolutely nothing that's useful. Her e-mail today was with the curator of a museum in a small Midwestern city that wants to exhibit, in two years time, her rooms. Hagar knits rooms. Or has knit at least one room and apparently is planning to knit more. I saw it. It was enormous. Blood red walls of yarn with a floor of yarn and a sofa and two chairs of yarn big enough to sit on. It was all one piece—an environment I guess you would call it—that hung from the ceiling in a large gallery and which, if you took off your shoes, you could walk into. I did that and the experience was, well, it was grand. That's the word I used to describe it to Hagar when she asked, but privately I thought it too gynecological. The red stringy softness made me think of female things. Earthy and organic are qualities I obviously like, but this felt like a visit to the uterus. Which is discomfiting, making you feel as though you were peeping up close on a couple in the midst of . . . or hearing a couple in the midst of . . . I wanted abstraction. And maybe that's the direction she'll go in. Maybe the rooms will lose the realism of blood and furniture and take in the wider sweep: fear, mortality, homeland. Who knows?

As Lily sucks, I can see the muscles working in her cheek. She turns her head to look at me from the safety of her mother's arms, milk glistening on her chin, the wet, pointed nipple exposed. She turns back, slides it into her mouth, and the muscles in her cheek start again.

"It will require an extensive body of work," Hagar is saying. "But how can I turn it down? So I said yes. Even though, God knows, our lives are really going to have to change, and for this little one I'm afraid we'll have to find a sitter because I'll need more than nights. I'll need to be working on my days off too."

She turns to me point-on and this time there is only one message and it is very clear. But babysitting is a question I can't address just yet because as the warm autumn sun beams on us I am filled with rage. It all fit, didn't it? Befriend the lonely woman at the top of the hill because one day she will be useful. Babysitting! How very lovely. And fast on the heels of babysitting, old age and boredom.

Hagar switches Lily to the new breast and the used one peeks at me, its peaceful face unmasked. Little does it know that the days of such beauty are numbered. The milk ducts will shrivel, the lift will drop, and the whole pillowy mass will cave in. As Lily's lips latch onto the new nipple, I remember that feeling. Nothing in this world fits us like those practiced gums. Richard's mouth is good and nice and necessary, and I do miss it, but there is nothing that locks so securely, that has such clear prerogative as those hard toothless gums.

Suddenly, I could not sit there. I saw my hand opening the door, my foot entering the kitchen, and I knew exactly who I was. I would not do it. The answer was no. No to all of it. I would not be a part of her scheme. The word they use now is enable and I grabbed it greedily. Yes, I would not enable her. She was the one with the milky tits. Let her take care of her baby.

"I'm really sorry," I said, coming back out as though I'd simply gone in for the bathroom. "I'm sure you'll find someone. There are lots of people who would jump at the chance, I'm sure, and you can keep me in reserve for emergencies. But on a daily basis, I just have too much to do around here." I looked out at my landscaping, but we both knew that come November everything would be under snow and my days would be free. "And, if I could be truthful, there's something I've been meaning to say. If you don't mind getting some advice. It's just that, Lily's going to grow up quickly, faster than you can imagine, and this wonderful time, this time when she's so dependent, maybe it makes better sense to be with her now, when she needs you, and save the art for when she starts school. And maybe my job, as your friend, is not to enable you."

Hagar was gathering her things. "Thank you for the internet."

My cheeks are hot, my skin buzzes with embarrassment. I hear her car start, the tires slip on the gravel, and by the time I follow her outside, the battered green station wagon has already rounded the curve.

Well, it's her problem. If she wants to take offense, let her. The last of the sun melts into the western horizon and in the east, the fat orange face of a harvest moon is balanced ridiculously over the trees. It leers at me. Okay, okay, so maybe it isn't only her problem. I can cede that much.

That's when I remember the yellow hallway. And there in the hallway is Richard's grandfather. I see the playful look on his face, the thin, whiskery cheeks, the surprisingly full and fleshy lips. "How did it happen?" he asks.

When he takes my hand, I feel his smooth dry palm, his knobby fingers. I feel it as unmistakably as though I were still there. And then I realize: he is not resisting this. He is eighty-seven and he is simply surprised.

So I call, but of course she does not answer the phone. Why are women so complicated? I will have to get in the car and drive over. But I know she won't come to the door. I will have to open it myself. Hagar! I will shout, stepping into her house, I have come down from the hill to tell you something! The drama of that announcement will summon her. But her eyes will flash like heat lightning. She will not let it go. Please, I will say in a soft voice, Don't be offended. I am in no position to give advice to anybody. I am old.

That's what I want to tell her. Those three short words are so new in my mouth I will have to say them again. I am old. But I don't know the first thing about it.

American Pictures

Apparently, his father had tried to drive himself to the hospital, but the pain was so bad he'd asked the neighbor to drive him instead. At the hospital, he'd asked the nurse to call his son. That had been twelve hours ago, and on the whole trip up from the city, subway to the bus, seven hours on the bus, and then an hour's drive in his father's car, Dan's chest had felt like a tree with a roosting turkey startling up through its branches. It was a commotion all country kids knew, and it sat in his body, mile after mile, tires rolling down the black roads, until he stepped off the elevator onto his father's floor.

But his father was alive. There was nothing to fear, not yet, and when the nurse took him to the room, he set down his bag, pulled out a chair, and waited for her to leave before he dared look at the figure in the bed. Alive. But clearly, only just. The body was flattened. The mouth was open, the expression mindless. On the console next to the bed a line zig-zagged across a screen. The room was hot. He shrugged out of his jacket and sweater, then searched under the blanket for his father's hand, but when he closed his fingers around it, nothing changed on the face.

His father's hand was useful, more useful than his own would ever be. It knew its way around engines. How to adjust a carburetor, clean a spark plug, lubricate, tighten, replace. He stroked the skin on the back of the hand with his thumb, feeling all the hours of anticipation settle into numbness. What he had feared had finally arrived, but he could see right away that this extreme would be different than the others because his father, unlike his mother and sister, had achieved the expected age for a mortal event.

When he was little, his friend Colby had shot a wild turkey out of season. They'd dragged the body out from the thickets, and when the involuntary movements ceased, they'd plucked the feathers. They'd scraped the innards just as they'd seen their fathers do, then they covered the raw, pitiful thing with a blanket of leaves and built a fire over it, squatting under the winter sky, nursing the flame one stick at a time, smoke climbing the frosty air. They roasted it all morning and when they poked it out of its bed it was a greasy, black, burnt ghost of itself, and though the charred meat took a lot of chewing, it was good. The burnt parts had the salty flavor of fire; the meat tasted like leaves. They sucked the bones, passing the carcass between them, telling each other the only thing they lacked was whiskey. But they were nine years old and the romance of their fathers' worlds hadn't yet translated to action. Not that Dan's father ever drank; he disdained anything soft or easy, but Colby had seen it first-hand most weekends. He had watched how the bottle caused a bloom of liveliness and in high school he would be the one to bring drugs back to their village.

"Dad?"

Now that he had arrived, the bird in his chest was finally settled. A hen turkey, he decided. She folded her long, tattered wings, tucked her beak under feathers, and found the right place on his rib bone to rest. The same one, the same young hen they had eaten.

"Dad?"

There was no sound. But it wasn't like his father to sleep so trustingly. He was the one who woke at every disturbance, a cat in heat, a chipmunk running cross the attic, a son's late return. He liked to joke that he was his own best guard-dog. That's how he had known when Dan was getting into trouble in high school. And that's how his father had stopped him. He knew about his sister too, but maybe he had lacked the courage to demand a change. So he must have known when their mother had strayed, but that too he let pass. Maybe he had less certainty with the women. But when his boy went out with the wrong people, and weekend after weekend, the cars pulled up to drop him off and the last one, the final one, drove off before his son could even get himself through the door, he made his demand. "You got to stand on your own two feet and be solid. You're it! You're the only one left." He remembered the long leathery finger raising itself out of the bathrobe pocket, coming through the air to stab his sternum.

He was hungry. His only food had been candy bars from the bus stations on the road, and he couldn't stomach any more sweetness. He closed his eyes and let the day catch up to him. Unlike his father, Dan slept deeply and in any situation, a sofa, a chair, a seat on the subway, he could disappear into sunken, comfortless oblivion. Once, when a girl took him back to her apartment, he fell asleep on her coach before they even got to her bedroom. So she assumed he wasn't interested. And maybe he hadn't been. There were times when sex scared him. Particularly if it was a desperate kind of a woman. He was attracted to the cool ones, the ones it was a challenge to get to know, because the easy ones reminded him of the women in his family, his mother and sister, two females who had ignited hot and burned up quickly.

His mother had died when a small plane piloted by a man no one knew crashed into a hillside. Nothing to explain it: the weather calm, the fuel tank full, and the man, probably her boyfriend, an experienced pilot.

Evelyn blazed out on reckless driving and for that event there were too many facts. She had been sixteen. They pulled the car from the ravine; she was the one at the wheel, fully dressed, while the boy next to her was naked. His father, not a man who ever had money to spare, wrote a check for three hundred and seventy five dollars to the reporter to hold back that embarrassing fact. So Dan didn't find out till high school when any swill about anyone was slopped around.

Neither death was "honorable," his father's word, so his father didn't miss a day at the garage and wouldn't allow his son to miss school. It passed. The worst of anything always passed.

When Dan jolted awake, he was thinking about money. The bus ticket had wiped him out. There had been enough gas in his father's car to get him to Dansville, but he was counting on the old man to have a couple of twenties. Otherwise, he didn't know what they would do because all Dan had was a five.

First, he'd started the car. Then he'd gone into the house. The back door, as always, was unlocked, and when he turned on the fluorescent, the kitchen was a mess, dishes piled on the counter, boxes of food sitting on the table, chili or something in a pan on the stove. The toilet was running in the bathroom. He jiggled the handle to get it to stop and then he checked the Webster's sitting on the bookcase in the hallway where his father hid cash. He turned to the word "field," and all he saw was a five. He grabbed it, figuring his dad had taken the rest when the neighbor ran him to the hospital. But it was strange about the kitchen. His father hated mess. He was neat and scrupulously frugal, storing every scrap of food in the fridge till it rotted. Unlike Dan who consumed and tossed like a man with no tomorrows.

He went back to sleep because it was night still, and dreamed that his father's 1966 Pontiac Bonneville, now parked outside at the Dansville hospital, roared down the street, carrying his father away. That was the other odd thing. His father prided himself on keeping his ancient car in mint condition, but he hadn't replaced the muffler. Had he been in pain for a long time? Was that why things were neglected? When he woke again, light filled the room. Two orderlies were sliding the old man onto a gurney.

"Hey, wait a minute! Dad?"

He followed the gurney down the hall to the elevator. "Helicopter's waiting," the nurse informed him.

"Why? Where's he going?"

"Surgery's scheduled in Rochester."

"Rochester?" That was another hour, another half tank of gas. "Why can't they do it here?"

"Most surgeries are in Rochester. That's where the specialists are."

When he kissed his father's cheek, his eyes blinkered open. The fingers slid out from the blanket and, as the gurney was pushed into the elevator, they waved. Dan squeezed in as the door slid closed, but the nurse stopped it, made him get out.

"Sorry, restricted area. Only hospital personnel." She took him to the nurse's station where she typed at a monitor and gave him a printout with the name and location of the bigger hospital. It was all the way on the north side of Rochester, and gas was going to be a problem. Last month, he'd snipped his credit card into a million pieces. End of temptation. Nothing on the debit card: he'd been out of work and the new job was so new it hadn't paid yet.

"Fuck!" He hissed it with such vehemence it should have attracted notice, but everyone at the nurses' station was occupied. He walked into the lounge and banged the Coke machine, imagining the canned, comic jangle of quarters into the change cup, but the steady illuminated face gave nothing. He and Colby, the same winter as the turkey feast, had tested all the soda machines in the village, two at the gas station, one at the village office, and at 2:00 a.m. they imagined that their sharp, precise kicks would knock loose some kind of gate on the inside and all the sweet money the machines hoarded would fall into the cup faster than they could grab it with their chubby hands. It didn't work, but defeat gave them the giggles. Dan's mother had died the year before; Colby's mother was about to disappear, and crazy laughter in the freezing dark night on an empty street where nothing moved except the pink rat's tale of an opossum sliding under a wood pile, was the only way to announce their collusion with badness. He didn't laugh now, but the machine's vivid colors inspired the same rage.

There was a chapel down the hall. He hated religion. He hated its presumption of authority. He didn't believe in God and was suspicious of the Bible; all it seemed to do was advocate for terrible things. *Interdenominational.* That word was over the door. Right, he thought, but none of the books of other religions were any better. He peeked inside. The lighting was muted and the carpet and two short pews were bathed in the default beige of public places. There was a piece of stained glass, but it was a false window, he could see the bulb behind it, and the design was abstract and meaningless. A woman with long brown hair sat in the first pew, but he ignored her. Now he wondered if perhaps she could help.

"Excuse me."

She looked up.

"Are you the minister or something?"

"Sure."

That confused him. Either she was or she wasn't. "I mean, are you?"

"Yes, and I give free counsel."

He stepped inside. "Meaning what?"

"I'm an artist. The doctor's with the person I was visiting and I can't stand TV and it's always on in there." She nodded towards the lounge.

He smiled at that. "Yeah, I hate TV too," he lied, remembering all the hours he'd been spellbound. TV had been a more dependable, and later, the only mother in his and Evelyn's childhood, and on days they were home alone, its disorder had been the most reliable order they had. "Hey.... listen, could you loan me like eighty bucks? I've got to drive to Rochester.

My dad was just flown up there for emergency surgery and I have his car and I'm out of cash, this was so unexpected, and I have to fill the tank. I swear I will send you a money order when I get home. I swear I will pay you back. I know you probably don't have eighty dollars, but maybe you could ride with me to the gas station and put a tank on your card? My debit card's empty and I...." but he knew he couldn't tell her about his credit problems.

"What's he up there for?"

He looked at the paper he was holding. "Neuro something. I think it's his stomach. He has terrible ulcers."

"May I look?"

He watched her eyes read the unintelligible phrases. She was pretty. She had a clean, fresh face and smart eyebrows, smart eyes. Her mouth was a no-nonsense mouth, not a pouting mouth, a serious straight-on mouth that would talk straight to you, maybe. And the hair that just hung there. She didn't touch it. She didn't fling it or swish it or do anything but ignore it. So it just sat there on its own, in its own amber light.

"I don't know what it is either. They didn't tell you?"

"I know this is really bizarre, but I just got here. So I haven't spoken to any doctors."

"Well, you have to get to Rochester, don't you? Come on."

Daniel Field was used to people giving him the finger. Bosses, girlfriends, buddies, the woman at the makeshift office where he volunteered after 9/11—the finger manifested as any number of disappointments—a check that never came, a call that wasn't returned, a job that was only a rumor. So he was prepared. In fact, maybe it was the presumption of failure that allowed the growing absurdity of his attempts. On the long bus ride up there he'd figured out some things, mostly his foolishness. Like eighty dollars, how ridiculous was that?

So he wasn't surprised when she disappeared. But then, there was a little exhale in his brain, something like the whoosh on a cell phone when a message comes in, and he replayed it: *You have to get to Rochester, don't you? Come on.*

After they gassed up, she slipped into the front seat next to him though the hospital was only two blocks away. Then he remembered that people who lived in rural places never thought about walking. So he pressed the gas and the engine roared. "The funny thing is that my dad is a mechanic, a really good one," he said because he was embarrassed about the muffler. Last night, when the roar had filled the empty garage, it seemed a sure sign that his father was lost. Now, as he steered the noisy car in the direction of the hospital, he was hopeful.

"Where are you going?"

"Your friend? The doctor's probably done, right?"

She laughed. "Doesn't matter. I was ready to leave anyway. I'm going to move on."

"Oh yeah? Well, just give me your address and I have the receipt and like I said..."

"Could you take me to Rochester? Drop me off downtown?"

"You don't have a car?" He was beginning to think she was just as shiftless as he was. And he didn't need that kind of baggage, not now. He was done with that type. He had to take care of his father.

"I got a ride down and I would love to get a ride back. I would be extremely grateful. Could you drop me off on Goodman Street?"

But he didn't want to get off the expressway. He wanted to go straight to the hospital.

She must have felt his hesitation because she said, "Or I could come to the hospital with you. I could help."

"Well, that's the thing, I don't need help. I've got to do this on my own. Things are kind of rough right now, okay?" The turkey slapped its wings. The sudden noise, the absurdity of a large bird sitting in the top of a tree. He wanted to leave the woman in Dansville.

On the highway, they didn't speak even though they could have. With speed, the muffler was quiet. All at once, she made a sudden movement and he startled, as though she were going for a gun, as though she were some kind of a crazy person. But she was just reaching for the canvas bag she'd thrown onto the back seat when she first got in. It was too large for a purse, and from the corner of his eye seemed to be more like a suitcase. He saw a hairbrush, some socks. Then she pulled out a camera. "Do you mind if I take your photo?"

"Ah, I don't think so. No pictures." What was she? Some kind of undercover agent? Going after Colby's friends? Was he dealing even now, even in the VA?

"Okay, no argument." She put the camera back into the bag and tossed the bag over the seat again. "Photos are not so good in a car anyway. It will be better at the hospital."

"No photos, please. Not anywhere." She was some kind of narcotics agent and since he was Colby's oldest friend, he was maybe a prime suspect. They should leave the poor sucker alone. The poor pathetic….

"No photos? But that is my purpose. American Pictures, it's a full half of my project. May I tell you about it?"

"Look, I'm really sorry. But I lost my job; I have no money; my dad's in trouble. No photos, okay? I'm really kind of a fuck-up right now."

"What do you mean, fuck-up?"

The question seemed impossible. "Who are you? A fuck-up? You're looking at one. So *you* tell *me*, what is it?"

He said it in anger but she took the question seriously. "A man of many loose ends, maybe? Not quite certain he is okay? I don't know, something like that?"

"Seriously, where have you been, Tanzania?"

"I have been away, though not Africa. I've been in France actually, speaking French for the last maybe dozen years? So my idioms, they're a little rusty."

"France, huh? Why France?"

"I am a dual citizen. French and American. My mother American, my father French, and my project is to compare the cultures. Make a book. In America, which is a land of no, no, no, no, many, many no's, I meet people and I say yes and I see where that takes me. I document each person I talk to with photos. I started in Atlanta, Georgia, and now I am in Rochester, New York. One person at a time. My journey is determined by nothing but casual encounters, and at the end of a year in America and then a year in France, there will be a gallery show and a book. That is my hope."

"So what's this say yes thing about?"

"Well…" there was a pause while she looked at the road ahead of her. "Saying yes is about the simple act of saying yes."

"That's not telling me a whole hell of a lot." The line had sailed into his mind, tone and everything, and before it was out of his mouth he realized it had been spoken to him not even twenty-four hours ago when he couldn't answer any of the questions put to him by his boss. Hospital, emergency, father: what more did he want?

Specifics, it turned out, like appendix, stroke, infection. But Dan didn't know. The hospital hadn't run the tests. That's why he needed to be there.

Unfortunately, the boss hadn't heard about the *Say Yes* campaign. "Listen, Field, I'm not making *this* up. This is the truth. When you get back from your little vacation don't bring your ugly mug to any of my parking lots. We're finished, got it?"

It didn't put her off. So when she asked with a brightness that seemed absurd, "Where did you come from?" he didn't just say The City. He elaborated a little, "downstate, you know, Brooklyn," just to show that he was grateful. Then, for some reason he couldn't fathom, he gave her the whole run-down, going to New York after 9/11, feeling like he needed to help because of the same thing in his life, the plane, the crash, losing someone in such a sudden and inexplicable way. But after a few months he began to notice that they always gave *him* the brute jobs and the college kids the desk-work, the answering-phones-stuff. So he stopped showing up. Let the rich kids ruin *their* lungs too. But he'd stayed in the city, moving from one couch to another, trying to save enough to rent an actual corner of a room somewhere, and getting nothing but shitty jobs, the last one the lowest so far, parking cars for a parking lot empire, and having no luck at anything, all of it falling apart.

"It doesn't take luck."

"Yeah, I guess not, I guess that's kind of a lousy excuse, but what does it take? Because it seems to me every other person I know… And they weren't even volunteers. I was a volunteer, but nothing matters, nothing helps. I vacuumed basements, heavy industrial machines, a hundred basements. They owe me, you know?"

"It takes being confident, but also realistic. You must claim to be someone who is dependable and responsible, and then be that dependable and responsible person, not slide back into *I was a volunteer*. Do you take offense at correction? That might be a problem."

He was about to say, look, I don't need your therapy. But the Pontiac was flying them towards Rochester, smoothly, quietly, and he felt proud of his dad for keeping such an impossible, outdated machine alive so he said instead, "How do you know these things?"

She laughed. "I watch and listen. It's a difficult task. You might think it sounds easy, but I can tell you it is very, very hard. You must empty yourself of all…what do I want to say? Opinion? No, not just that, all preconception, all expectation. My project is based on listening and looking and being kind. I don't put my photos on Facebook or Instagram. I'm saving them for a formal art show and then a book, American pictures in one half, French pictures in the other. But if that doesn't happen, it's okay. I am changing the world slowly, modestly, one person at a time, through believing, giving, making things possible. Opening doors, not closing them. I am an ambassador of kindness."

He smelled a scam. "Why?"

"Why?" she repeated, her tone incredulous. She turned towards him, facing him square-on, eyes wide open. "It is this!"

It was so fucking intimidating he could hardly drive.

"This! Do you feel it?"

Clearly, she was into the hard sell, an idea, a membership, he wasn't sure. But there was nothing in her hands. And that bag of hers, it was stuffed with possessions. She was a vagrant. Or an FBI undercover guy.

"Surely you can feel it? The line of sympathy between us? We are connected as human beings."

"Connected?" he asked, stalling for time. And as he might have predicted, there was the full-on gaze. "You must take me for an idiot." That line, too, was borrowed. From where, he couldn't remember.

"Ah, non, vraiment! I trust you."

"Listen, I don't speak French."

The familiar landscape flew past. It was the same fields and farms and outlying buildings he remembered from all the times he'd driven up to Rochester for movies and concerts with friends, the same steely grey sky as every other winter. They passed the sign for Geneseo. Good old Geneseo, home of the state college, location of the means and methods of one hundred ways of getting wasted. Colby knew all the bars, all the contacts. He'd had an inside man, a Manhattan connection, in one of the dorms.

They passed Avon, Rush. A fog of white lay over the fields. It was a huge, sucking, whirling space, home of deer and turkey, the snow printed with their steady traffic. A hawk, sitting on a wire, scanned for rodents, and the subdued light, its endless horizon, endless sameness, endless soul-sucking opacity glared down from the sky as it had always done. As it had done for his mother and sister, two people who had been desperate for excitement. If you thought about it, and he had, it wasn't a coincidence that their deaths had happened in March when it was still winter, still sleeting and snowing, when the accumulated cloud cover from all of the lakes in their area, Finger Lakes to the east, Lake Erie to the west, Lake Ontario to the north, hung over the weary, ice scarred land. Colby had enlisted in March; that wasn't a coincidence either. It was the kind of unchanging light, day after day, that hammered you down, a light that had no surprises. Sliding along the highway beneath it, he realized this was why he stayed in the city even though the rents were so punishing. There was sun down there. There were whole days, and not just a single day here and there, but a whole stretch of them, one after another, with winter sun. And even when it was cloudy the sun broke through for a little while.

The rusted bridges and concrete pillars on the southern edge of Rochester seemed unequal to the task of holding up the road, but they did, the interchanges appeared, and as they entered the city, their highway merged with others. He chose the ramp he thought was correct.

"Right, 390 north."

"You know everything don't you?"

"Well, I'm getting to know you and I'm getting to know Rochester. That's not everything."

"But how do you know me?" She didn't, she couldn't, and though he might be hidden, he wasn't anybody's supplier.

"You could know *me* if you tried. You don't try, that's all. You're all taken up with you. But you could observe some things about me if you gave yourself the opportunity. Not when you're driving though. Later. When we're in the hospital."

"I thought I was taking you to Goodman Street."

"I'd like to come with you to the hospital."

He didn't respond. The thing he'd learned, when his mother had died, then his sister, when Colby came back without his feet, is that what you thought about something didn't matter. The beast of nightmares had an endlessly rich imagination. Including, right there next to him, the ambassador from France.

They waited outside of surgery. A man came through the doors in the booted, hatted, baby-blue uniform of the operating room and asked for Family of Field, and Dan stood up. "That's me."

"I'm sorry," the doctor said, "but there are complications. You folks might as well stretch your legs because it's going to be awhile longer."

There was a splatter of blood on the doctor's blue top and Dan knew it was his father's. He imagined the surgery, the steel tables, the gutters draining fluids, the thick grey coil of intestines pulsing under the lights. There was a flash of silver, latex covered fingers peeling back skin.

"Are you hungry?" the girl asked. He followed her to the cafeteria, squeezing into the elevator with hospital employees, saying to the beast, *Please, I will be good. Just bring him back.* Was it a prayer?

He bought a roll and a pat of cold butter. It cost two dollars plus change, leaving him with enough for a Red Bull, but he decided to start being good right then and not give in to his craving. So he drew a glass of water. Then he sat down across from her, accepting her presence, maybe even glad of it, and proud of the fact that he had paid for his food. Prayer was new for him. Hope was too. He'd never held hope for very long, and though he wasn't hungry, he made himself eat. He made himself drink the entire glass of water, just like a mother. Sometimes he had to do that, become the mother he never had, someone to make sure he wore clean clothes and ate breakfast. Sometimes he didn't bother.

"I think we should talk," she said. "But not now, over food. Let's go back up, see if he's in recovery, and then we can find the chapel. That's the secret, you know. Hospitals have chapels and bathrooms and cafeterias. You can live in them easy and nobody pays attention."

He did not trust her. And he saw no reason to talk. All he had to do was get through these next few days and then he could get back to the sun, back to civilization. Even if he had to take his father with him. (But where would they live? How could they afford anything down there? You couldn't surf couches with a depressed old man. Weren't there places for poor people? The farthest reaches of Queens? Some little basement apartment beyond the subway, reached only by bus?)

The chapel at Rochester General was larger. It looked less like a church because there wasn't any schmaltzy stained glass or pews, just a row of chairs in the front and a sofa with a reading light along the back wall. They sat there.

She began: "In America, everything stops you. What is the word? Thwart. Everything thwarts you. You need a lot of money just to go to the doctor, just to go to college. Huge amounts of money. The food is terrible, but that's beside the point. People everywhere are beaten-down, unhappy. Or else they're drunk and high. Everyone's expectation is that the answer will be no, that the desire to do something, to go somewhere, to accomplish something will be thwarted. So I say yes. That's my guiding principle. I have no plan, no purpose, but that. I say yes in every encounter. Though not every. I'm careful. I don't say yes to things that would be harmful to me or to someone else, but I do take risks. I take risks by trusting people, choosing to believe what I am told."

"You get paid? Someone gives you a credit card and like, no restrictions?"

"It is me. I fund it. But don't let that distract you. I'm here with you. And right now I want to tell you what I see." She paused. He felt the turkey rustle its wings.

"Nobody ever comes clean. It's too risky. But I have nothing to lose because I don't care if you like me or not. Also, I will never see you again. So it doesn't matter. You will never find a person as honest as me, or who knows as much about you. I mean, not everything, only certain knowledge, only what I see on your face. I don't know anything about your life experience except for what I see on your face."

She had an encouraging, eager expression, entirely cleansed of judgment; he felt as though he needed to protect his eyes, as though her face was a wattage he couldn't bear.

"May I take your photo now?"

Again, he hesitated.

"You are very beautiful, but in a rough, unpretty way, very boy. Very boy," she repeated, the wattage softening. "No one has ever loved you enough. And I think you have never loved back. Without regrets, without hesitation. You have, I think, many..." she paused. "Not regrets, that's not the right word. No, I think many insecurities. Maybe, what is it, guilt? But you are not guilty. You have nothing to be ashamed of. You hold your family close to you, Dan, I can see that, your father especially. What I think, and of course I don't know, but what I think is that when you choose to love someone you will become a strong person. That eighty dollars is for you. It is from me in gratitude for letting me take your photo."

"But I didn't say that you could." And then he got angry. "Hey, I said I was going to pay it back."

"It is a gift." Her eyes were shiny, like she was about to cry. Some kind of a spirit, that's what she was. "Listen, I have given you a gift. Accept it." She took the camera out of her bag. "May I?" He nodded a yes. But she said, "Please, for me, express it like you mean it."

"What?"

"Like you really want me to take your picture. Like you want to be generous."

"Okay." He got down on his knees as though he were a penitent. "Will you please take my picture?"

Clicking, dancing about him, she talked: "Dan Field, a man of, well I don't know how old you are, let's say twenty five years, that I met in Dansville, New York who took me to Rochester, New York. That will be the caption. Nothing more. I will not reveal anything but that. It's all simple. Very, very simple. Dan Field received a gift from Brigitte Robeau." She squatted down, then she stood on a chair, then she lay on the floor and looked up at him. He could tell she was experienced, but still, there was a dark, dusty corner of suspicion in his mind: "Listen, if this is about Colby Danvers I want you to know that ever since he came back, I've only seen him a couple of times. I'm not his man in the city. Search me, there's nothing on me. And I really don't think he's dealing anymore. Leave the poor son of a bitch alone why doncha."

"Colby Danvers? Do you suggest I go see him?"

"He's in Bath. At the VA."

"Which is what?"

The question was so open, so guileless he said, "Never mind."

That night he stayed at a house in Rochester where everyone spoke French. They fed him and gave him a couch to sleep on. In the morning, he left his phone number and e-mail with Brigitte in case the book were ever published. He signed a form that gave her permission to use his image and then he drove back to the hospital on surface streets, the rumble announcing every touch on the throttle.

On the sixth floor the hallway was so polished it gleamed and the doors at the end shimmered with light. His father looked just as pale and exhausted, but now he was hooked up to more machines than before. Dan tried to give him a solid hug, but it was difficult with all of the wires.

The old man's lips parted to say something. "Thirsty," he whispered, lifting a bruised hand to point to the bed-table.

Dan saw a Styrofoam cup filled with ice water and held it under his father's mouth. He put the straw to his mouth but nothing happened. Then he moved to the bed and squeezed in behind his father's shoulders, supporting his back against his chest so his head was raised enough to sip. The skull was heavy and surprisingly warm and it bent forward, the lips sucking the water in a needy, desperate way. Dan gave him another cupful, and when he was done with the second cup, Dan settled his father's head back into the pillows.

"That was good," he whispered. "Thank you."

Mischief

1.

The call came in February. Chipper Hanson had found a lost goat and tied it to his porch, where it was kicking and butting and destroying things. He called the hardware, and the hardware called me, because if nobody got it off his porch soon, his wife was going to get the gun and take care of the problem herself, and whether that would involve just the goat or the goat *and* the husband, no one could say.

Right away, I offered to take him.

There was a foot of old snow, hard-crusted. The pickup was drifted in. I dug out the wheels and started scraping ice off the windshield, the hills echoing the noise. The thermometer registered seven degrees, the cold a razor against my cheeks. The sun had vanished, and the sky was hard, metallic. When I saw glass, I started the engine, ran the defrost to melt the rest, and went into the house for my purse. Ramona to the rescue!

Andover is three miles down the road, and all the way there it never occurred to me to wonder why, in a place where a lot of people had barns and animals, I was the one they called. All I knew about were chickens. But Jim at the hardware must have remembered that Shep and me were planning to get a couple of does in the spring.

The hardware was where we bought the fencing supplies. It was where we asked our questions. Of course, that was one of the strikes against us. We were city folk, ignorant about things the others grew up knowing, too willing to suppose they had the time to talk us through the way to do one thing or another, repair the hydrant, set a corner in fence line so it will hold.

So I was pleased when I picked up the phone that winter morning and a deep voice that I knew right away, belonging to the big-bellied man who'd sold us thirty rolls of woven wire last summer and recommended where we could buy locust posts, called me by my first name. He was a man whose family had starved and shivered for generations in a rundown old farmhouse at the top of one of the hills until, finally, the third son got out of dairying and opened the hardware that now employed his brothers too. This was the person who said, "Mona, there's a lost goat down here, and it's wrecking Chipper Hanson's porch at Twenty-Two Greenwood, where he got it tied, and we wondered if you and the boss could take it off of Chipper's hands—he don't got no barn—even if it's just for a little while."

Ah, but don't be fooled. It's not that I'm the world's most spontaneous person, not by a long shot! And I knew it would take time to dig out the truck. No, I agreed to it because Jim had called me "Mona". After the thousands of dollars we had spent at his store, after the advice he'd given and the questions we'd asked, I was still "Mrs. Brightner." Shep and me both, we were "The Boss" and "Mrs. Brightner." I'd given up ever becoming "Ramona" in this town.

We were different. The Boss had been to college, and they suspected (rightly) that I'd been, too—that is, real college, not a state techie. But the biggest problem? As superintendent of the school, Shep's salary was public information, and though it was modest compared to other places, it was, in Andover, quite a bit larger than most, and when all of those savers and scrimpers and government haters got their school tax bill every September, they resented us. "Mona" and "Shep" would never happen. I was resigned to it. But on that morning, "Mona" and "The Boss" was what Jim said, and it was as musical as the first robins in March. And on a bitter day in February, when the temperature hadn't climbed over ten degrees in a week and the sky's dark light was as even as a sheet of stainless steel, "Mona," better even than "Ramona," coming from Jim's mouth made me happy.

It was a small goat with a long, shaggy brown coat and long floppy ears. The floppy ears meant its mother or daddy was a Nubian, and the furred coat meant it had been living in the open for a while. The curious thing about it was the collar. It wore a necklace of green felt with tassels and triangles of red felt sewn onto it like a jester's costume. It was a homemade affair, some kind of Christmas getup. Had the goat escaped from a manger scene at a local church? Not in Andover, because Jim would have known about it. But maybe in Independence or Canisteo; no one would have thought a goat on the run could make it all the way here.

Chipper Hanson put his arms around the goat's legs and lifted it into the space behind my seat. He tied a rope from the necklace to the door handle, giving the animal just enough room to lift its head. "Gotta keep it tight, Mona. This one's got a taste of the wild. Been runnin' with the deer and thinks it's just one a them. Hope you got good fencing."

After he knotted the rope so it would stay, he stood at the open door, talking. His hair smelled like cigarettes, and his voice had a smoker's rich, syrupy tone. "See, I throwed 'em cracked corn. Out there." He nodded to the field behind his house. "First seed him, oh, maybe a week ago. And this morning, wouldn't you know it, just happened to look out, and the little bustard trottin' down the sidewalk just like he one a them kids going to school."

"'Him'? It's a him?" People had told us male goats were mean and smelly, and we had decided we only wanted does.

"Nah." He spit phlegm into the gutter. "Not him. He been robbed of his treasure. He's a choirboy, which in goats it's called a wether. See now..."

Chipper leaned in over the seat and, despite the cold, gave me a lesson on the psychology of the neutered male goat. "They got the male impulse, but they don't got the equipment. So wethers is orn'ry. Never did like 'em. Same hormones but no way to express themselves. So you and the boss, you got to watch it with this guy." He stepped away, slamming the door. He lifted a palm in thanks, and then he leaned towards me again, opening the door a crack, and said, "Tell you one thing: any longer and the wife would have shot me and the goat together. That's a new railing. The little bustard kicked out the spindles."

Sometimes I just felt lucky. Here I was, living in this beautiful, uncrowded place. I did farmwork. I could fling a fifty-pound hay bale onto the top of a high load easily as any man. I had a pickup to haul a goat. He sat quietly, though when we passed a house and he heard barking dogs, he *baa*ed a little goat *baa*, which is like a sheep's but more insistent. "Been running with the deer?" I said. "Then you should know about dogs."

I put fresh bedding down and filled a water bucket. Then I led him back to the barn and closed him into the stall with some hay. I planned to keep him locked up for a few days till he knew his home.

In the afternoon, I shoveled snow out of the truck and drove to the feed store, where they loaded me up with more bales of hay, a hayrack to hang on the wall of the stall, a rubber drinking bucket, and feeding dishes. By the time I got back, the sun was sinking, and my portion of the sky was flushed an encouraging pink.

But I will admit, as the kettle was heating for tea, the thought crossed my mind: I should have discussed it with Shep. No, he was meeting with the school board, and I had seen to everything. All Shep would have to do was hang the feeders and hayrack. I was no good with carpentry, and Shep was quick and efficient.

So I decided instead to tell our children. Two e-mails went out while the leaves steeped: one to Arianna, who was in college, and one to Lincoln, who worked as a contractor. "Got Goat." Nothing more. A tease to get them to call.

I toasted some bread, peeled a couple of hard-boiled eggs, and poured a large cup of tea. The first pause in the day. It's this, I've always thought, that marks the difference between us and the animals. Up in his stall, the goat was not reviewing the events of his last ten hours. He was eating, drinking, looking, listening, all at the same time, but I doubted that he was thinking about what had happened.

Or it could be a glass of wine or a cigarette, but it was all the same, an excuse for the chance to sit down. Had I done the right thing? Was it foolish to take on so much, so quickly, just because a villager had called me by my name? I started to see the situation from Shephard's point of view, remembering how difficult these last few weeks had been for him, first meeting with the state officials over the low test scores and now the school board over the budget.

Tomorrow he had to drive five hours for another meeting in Albany. And I knew he hadn't been sleeping well. A rogue goat was the last thing he needed. A rogue goat foisted on him by me. At exactly the wrong time. An escape artist. A male creature with no equipment. All my accomplishments were in the wrong direction. I had only made more complicated our already complicated lives.

I'd heard about Shephard Brightner long before I ever met him. In the small coastal town in Maine, twenty years ago, there was a group of women who passed his name around like a favorite recipe. Most were divorced, but a few, like me, had never been married. Didn't matter. Everyone was thrown together, and two very different populations congregated in the food co-op: the wealthy who had been enticed there by lots of things, the ocean being just one of them, and the others who depended upon the wealthy for their jobs. I was going to massage school; Shep was working as a contractor while he finished his degree. The both of us rented tiny places in the center of town, mine in an attic of someone's summer mansion, Shep a garage apartment, and commuted the hour to the city. To us it made sense; we like small-town life.

The first time I saw him, Shephard was on the stage at the high school. The town was having a referendum. Should the local school be closed and the kids bussed to the larger school in the next town, or should the local school be funded at greater taxpayer expense? Most people were for closing the school and bussing the kids. It seemed like a done deal. Then Shephard walked to the podium. People got quiet even before he said anything. The auditorium was packed, but I swear he looked at each person. The man had presence. He was just a contractor, a student at the university, but it was evident that he had the authority everyone else had lacked. His was a natural authority, an ability to know how to speak to a very particular group of people: lobster fishermen who were tough and independent, executives who were tired and simply wanted to eat the lobster and play golf, and then all of the in-betweens, the people like me with no money or steady job but loads of ideals. He began with a joke. I don't remember now what it was, but after we all had a laugh, he got serious.

First he showed us one way to look at the issue, and then he showed us another, and then he stated the conclusion he came to, and he made it seem so clear and obvious, we had no choice but to agree with him. It would be cheaper, he told us, and the kids would have more curriculum choices, but they would lose their identity as a place, as a neighborhood of people who had gone to school together their whole lives and had known each other and their families for a long time. The hour-long bus ride at each end of the day, combined with losing the idea of who they were as a

community, bid him as a future parent, a future educator, to vote no.

Someone in the first row stood up and started to clap. A wave of feelings swept over the room, and soon we were all on our feet, clapping and whistling and stomping. He had expressed the reservation that we all had but were afraid wasn't legitimate: that the pocketbook shouldn't be the only thing we considered. Community was foremost. Who we were, where we lived. That we were friends and neighbors sharing a common place that we all loved, and that this common place was the healthy, solid uppermost fact of our lives and was for our children a source of identity and support. Let's not rob them of it.

I'm not a speaker. I'm not a very political person, even, but after he was finished, I felt fired up. I was ready to volunteer to do whatever I could to make sure that the small central school in the middle of our town stayed open.

So I joined the campaign, and over the next weeks, I went to all the communities in the district. And then, one day, returning from a nearby peninsula where we had distributed leaflets, I was with him in his beat-up old van, buckets of drywall mud rattling in the back. He pulled into a gas station, and I watched as he filled up.

Shep is a tall man with long legs, wide shoulders. He likes to wear corduroy jackets, even back then he did, and the pockets of the jackets are always bulging with pens and pencils and scraps of paper with things written on them. He's one of the few people who never watches the ground when he walks. He looks straight ahead, and on his face there is a wide-open expression. Shep is a happy person most of the time, and I could see it in that forward-looking expression. He has big feet and big hands, and they give him an awkwardness, like a perpetual teenager, even now that he has graying hair. He slid in and started the motor, but I said, "Hey, wait a minute," and pointed to the other end of the lot. "Pull over there, will you?"

He thought something was the matter. Tires needed air; woman needed bathroom. It never occurred to him that it could be anything else. That's when I understood that as smart and charismatic as this guy was, he was also incredibly stupid. Or else, blind. Because, back then, I was a good-looking woman. At least some of the time, which is all even the best

of us can hope to achieve. Before kids, before the wear and tear of life's situations, I was thin and elegant, and I had really strong hands. Now I'm a bit of a used article. My skin is weathered, and inside, I feel an intensity that wasn't there before. I think it's the loss of biological focus.

So I leaned towards him, and when he turned my way, I kissed him on the lips. Only once, lightly, sweetly. But he was surprised. He hadn't been expecting it or even thinking about it. That made me wonder. Did he have a girlfriend? If so, she was surely keeping herself scarce. Was he not attracted to me, to women? But he was. A few times, I'd caught him watching. So why hadn't he ever made the first move?

I've had cups of tea over that question. And I wonder about it still. A man with a clear trajectory, ready to move up the ladder in the field of education, an articulate man, a man who has strong hands too. Why would he hesitate?

Outside, the snow squeaked under a set of tires. A car door slammed. The outer door to our mudroom sticks when it's very cold, and now I heard it shudder open. I heard him set his briefcase on the floor, pull off his boots, and then he opened the door into the kitchen.

"'Got Goat'? What's that, a Muslim billboard?"

I realized, suddenly, how stupid I had been. In the age of e-mail, information moves quickly. Then I remembered that he'd been planning to talk to Lincoln that day.

"Got goat," I confirmed, walking towards him. We touched lips.

He took a beer from the fridge (this was how *he* created a pause in his day) and sat down at the table heavily. He sighed. Then he said, "Is someone going to tell me what this is all about?"

I should claim *that* as the moment when everything changed. Not the phone call. The phone call was simply the outside event that started things moving. It was the man in the beautiful brown wool suit we had bought at a thrift store in that town in Maine all those years ago, sitting at the table with his legs crossed, feet in the woolen socks I had given him on his last birthday, who announced the change with that question: *Is someone going to tell me what this is all about?*

He was clearly annoyed, but then he had never been anything but direct. In fact, I loved him for his directness. But no, it wasn't that. It was the word *someone* spoken in a house where there was only me.

When men reach their middle years, their cheeks get the rougher, more weathered patina of old cars. A woman's body collapses like a worn sofa, and if there's been loss, her face shows it. Shep's face had a look of forbearance.

"Everything's taken care of," I said. "There's nothing you'll have to do until the weekend."

"I'm going away this weekend."

"Isn't Albany tomorrow?"

"It is."

"So you'll be home Thursday night."

"No, I'm also going away this weekend."

When a husband makes a pronouncement like this to a wife he normally confides in, it startles. But there was nothing in the set of his mouth or the focus of his eyes that betrayed anything. I didn't say, *What do you mean?* I didn't say, *Where to?* I simply said, "Why?" And that's a curious thing. In a long marriage, in a small town that isolates us because of the political nature of Shep's job, we had been thrown together and, for many years, had been not only lovers but each other's only best friends. What I meant was: *Why would you go somewhere without me?*

He took a sip of beer. And then he didn't say anything. That hurt. Usually we're talkers. It came from all the different places we'd lived, from having to figure those places out quickly so both of us could function. School administration is a job about doing the right thing, but also making the opposition think it had been their idea. To be effective, you have to get the feel of a place quickly. And where to have a massage practice—that was the other delicate issue. It couldn't be in the town where Shep worked, but it couldn't be in a town where the people were going to think it was some kind of sex thing. Location is all-important. So when we first got to a new place, we ran the roads and went into bars, supermarkets, repair shops, gift emporiums—noticing, talking, introducing ourselves. Then we met and compared notes and made our conclusions together.

"I wanted to think things through on my own. For once, I wanted to act independently. That doesn't mean I want to be independent. I very much hope that you'll decide to join me later on."

Had I missed a connecting link?

"What are you talking about?" I sat down across from him. "Hey, will you please remember who I am?"

"Sorry. I was asked, very recently, to apply for a job as headmaster at a very prestigious private school in New Hampshire. It starts next fall, and apparently I'm their first choice, and they want me to come out this weekend to take a look. There's a slight cut in salary, but there's a huge cut in stress, and I'd be an independent educator." With a very straight face, he said, "In New Hampshire there's no Albany."

"You know it takes me a year to build up clients. Moving is a very big deal."

"They're more liberal in New Hampshire, more accepting of massage."

"But you're talking as though you've already accepted this."

"I haven't. I said I needed to come out and meet the trustees and see the place."

"But what about me? Where am I in all of this? Your partner. Hey, your partner!"

It seems to me that people are born with a certain level of ambition. None of us choose to struggle, but on the other hand, I don't think many of us choose to become president. Most of us simply want to be comfortable with an interesting job and a minimum degree of stress. But for me, were I to be truthful, I'd have to admit that my ambition is only to live in a small town and be known. Goats, chickens, a vegetable garden, and enough clients to keep me busy three days a week doing massage. That's it. So maybe Shephard's ambition balances my lack of it.

As we talked, I learned that it wasn't just a private school. It was the most distinguished private school in New England, if not in the entire United States, and though it looked like a slight pay cut on paper, in actuality it was a substantial raise, because housing, a beautiful and well-appointed Victorian mansion he showed me online, was part of the deal. No utility bills, no property tax, no federal standards, no state testing, no school board, no fundamentalists screening the classroom texts. This was the school that turned out the people who entered the highest levels of industry and government. Corporation presidents, senators. These were their alumni. And then there was me: Ramona the peasant.

That night, sitting in our kitchen, we were an island of light in the darkness. There are no shades or curtains on any of our windows. No reason for them. The nocturnal creatures—the deer, the fox, the opossum—are not Peeping Toms. I wanted him to meet the goat. But now, "Got Goat" seemed so wrong-headed I was ashamed to suggest it.

II.

I create lists. In grade school, I soothed myself with the sounds of things. There were the three ships Columbus brought to America: the *Niña*, the *Pinta*, the *Santa Maria*. I loved the perfect rhythm of those names and would say them over and over. I learned the three stars that make up Orion's Belt: *Alnitak, Alnilam, Mintaka*. They weren't as musical as the Spanish, but the Arabic was exotic.

As time went on, the list became a way to entertain my mind when I was at work. Nude, naked, unclothed: my hands kneaded those words into troubled skin. It is the perfect state of being, but occasionally, I'll get a woman who insists on wearing panties and bra. I guarantee, if she becomes a regular, she'll take those articles off. Not because I've said something, but because after a session she accepts herself. I never see my bodies in entirety; I see only parts. But I can deduce, and what I say to the foot and the shoulder is meant for the rest of it.

There are the three places Shep and I have lived—Blue Hill, Burlington, and now Andover—and the three states—Maine, Vermont, New York—that we've paid taxes to. We've chosen these places carefully, going only where there were opportunities for both of us. It is a fact, if you look at data, that superintendents move around. Ten years at one school, seven years at the next. The job is too political to last at any one place for very long. Of course, I choose to think Shep is different. I choose to be an idealist, to believe that despite the unrealistic, unfunded requirements of No Child Left Behind, despite school report cards and budget pressures, Shep will remain true to what he believes: that children learn in different

ways and that an effective school is one that uses a variety of teaching methods. But variety is more expensive, and when there are monetary pressures and a lot of hotheadedness, it's difficult to implement. These days he wakes up at 4:00 in the morning, and I hear him downstairs, pedaling his stationary bike, the chain making a clicking sound as he rides through the nighttime dramas that are a spillover of contentious days. It's good; it helps him survive. Because I want to stay here. I want to make this our home.

The turds are black; they drop out of the velvety anus like balls from a gum machine. They have no odor, because a goat's vegetarian intake is thoroughly digested by the time it exits, having been swallowed, processed in the rumen, then brought back up to be chewed some more as cud, swallowed again, and passed through the other stomachs, all of which are housed in the barrel suspended between the shoulders and the sharp, bony hips. Rumen, reticulum, omasum, abomasum: I say them to myself as I squat down in the stall. His breath is goaty, and he picks at my jacket with his soft, black lips and looks at me through flat, horizontal pupils. Clearly he's been with people, because he's comfortable with me, blows air against my neck, butts his head into my waist. I am learning the contours of his body, its little nicks and scrapes, as I pet him. I am sorry there aren't other animals in this barn, but at least he can hear the chickens in the neighboring shed, and when he goes out, they will keep him company. His long ears are soft, and though the rest of him is brown, they're light grey, almost white. His lashes are very long, also white, and the little teeth on his bottom jaw are small and straight. They nibble at my jacket sleeve, pull my glove out of my pocket. But his hoofs need trimming; he needs minerals. I need to buy these things. I also need to go to New Hampshire.

The feed store is at the top of the hill. As I moved through the shelves of animal supplies to the counter, a woman called out in a plucky voice, "What can we get you today?"

"Do you have minerals for goats?"

"Sure do. Comes in small and large."

"Do you have a hoof-trimming tool?"

"No, but let me get Joe." She laughed, and her voice dropped to a rasp. "Not that he's a hoof-trimming tool, but he's the one who will know."

"Wire cutters," Joe told me. "Ordinary wire cutters from the hardware store. They'll do it better." He had the same stocky build as the woman at the register. "How many goats you got?" he asked companionably.

When I told him the story, he whistled. "Wearing a jester collar in Christmas colors? If that critter been running since Christmas, he must be a mighty smart animal. Better watch out. He's gonna be hard to contain. And if he goes, best thing probably be to let him. He's a survivor, I'd say."

I found everything else I needed, and while I was paying for it, the door opened, letting in a gust of cold air, and a woman said, "You the one ordered this weather? Got to talk to you 'bout that."

"Hi, Darla!" the woman at the register called. To me she said, "That'll be twenty-two ninety-seven."

"Wasn't me ordered this weather," Joe chimed back. "Musta been Burdett."

"Then get that troublemaker out here now so's I can talk to him!"

I turned to look more closely at this woman who so effectively took center stage, and when my glance reached her eyes, she looked right back and said, "Ramona Brightner." She came towards me, holding out her hand. "Very pleased to meet you. We're neighbors. In a fashion. My two hayfields back onto your property. And I know Shephard. I'm Darla Oswald, head of the school board and a great fan of your husband." But then her attention turned. "There you are, Burdett! They tell me you're the one ordered this weather. You and me have a little talking to do."

An old farmer stood by the back door. "Just for you, Darla. I got a personal request line, straight to the almighty weather man, and I said very plainly, we want an old-time February, no climate change nonsense; we want nights below minus ten and days in the single digits. Kills the mosquitoes. Come on. You'll be grateful. Deep cold in the winter makes for a summer without pests. It's true. You wait and see." He hooked a hand in his overall strap. The other sleeve of his jacket was armless.

"What you need?" he asked without a pause, and she went into a long recitation of supplies.

I said, "So you're the one who makes all those round bales on the

field below us."

She cackled. "Yes, ma'am! Thirty rounds from either side of you, ten one field, twenty the other. You Brightners are a wedge right in the middle. Sort of strange. But way back, when it was all one piece, your acres must have been sold off to a relative. Made sense back then, and now, well, that's what we have to work with."

"I was wondering... I'm going to need hay, because I just got a goat. Next summer, could we buy some? Wouldn't need much. It's just one."

She threw her head back, blond hair tumbling, a gloved hand reaching up as she cried, "Oh no! Sweetheart, one goat will never do. They're herd animals. Just like horses. You have to have two or more." She pulled off her long black leather gloves—city gloves, not country gloves—and cackled again. "That's exactly how I started. Now I have twenty-three."

My first client that afternoon was a man who works outdoors as a surveyor. His body is starved for warmth, so I make the little room I rent behind the salon as warm as possible, and I set the electric pad on my table at high. I hold my hands in front of the heater before I touch him, and sometimes I set a hot, towel-wrapped rock in the middle of his belly or back while I massage his limbs. With him it's not emotional—it's body stress caused by wind and cold.

I am the only practitioner I know who doesn't use background music. Lots of people, as you work on them, have things to say, and silence gives them that chance.

Bruce likes to talk. Occasionally, he talks too much, but I'm not afraid to tell him when it's time to be quiet. He's a big man, six-three at least, and over two hundred pounds. He's also an ugly man. I don't know why that's important, but it makes me want to help him even more. I do a lot of work in the trapezius. I warm his shoulders, stroking and gliding, using smooth, continuous motions, talking to the muscles. I use all of my weight, pushing in, pulling back, working to loosen the fascia. His shoulders are big and meaty, tufted with hair. The oil darkens and flattens it, and when the skin is supple, I knead him like dough.

The room I rent is small and, as I explained before, very warm. I keep the light low and am very careful, as I move around the table, never to brush against his body, careful to keep it draped as I use knuckles and forearms along his spine, unlocking the tension. It still amazes me that in just an hour I can make this large, wind-battered man relaxed and pliant.

In the winter, Bruce comes once a week. He talks, mostly about his crew, the two or three kids he hired just out of college. He likes them. He loves them, actually, and seems, at least to me, to get too involved in their personal problems. But today he was talking about something else.

"You know the McCarthy place on Hartsville Hill? Been surveying it. Two hundred acres, all flat, with a stream, woods, and cleared portions. They're selling it off to speculators."

"Speculators?"

"For big bucks."

"What kind of speculators?" No one could be thinking of building a housing development in a place as isolated as Hartsville Hill.

"Gas. Marcellus Shale gas. You know about that, don't you?"

I try to keep the problems of the world out of my room, but they slip in regardless. "I've wanted to forget it," I told him. "I've been hoping that if I didn't pay attention it would go away."

"It's not going away; there's big money out there. There's leasing agents—they're crawling all over us right now, trying to get landowners to sign away mineral rights. And landowners, they're forming coalitions, because with contiguous acres they get better rates and a bigger signing bonus. You've heard of that, haven't you? The signing bonus? Hard to resist. A new truck, a new plow, a hydraulic splitter... you name it. Carries lots of temptation. The other kind of landowner, the one with principles, who wants solar or wind instead of the way drilling lays everything to waste, he's going to be outvoted. It contaminates the water. Or there's a good chance it will. You know that, don't you?" He paused. I gave an ambiguous murmur and continued knuckles along his spine.

"That signing bonus is so sweet. People are willing to risk it. And the one who isn't tempted, well, angry neighbors is just the beginning of his nightmare. Back in the Thirties we had an oil boom here, but shale gas, that's something different. Highly industrial. Mile-long wells, huge containment pools. Tanker traffic digging up roads. But the worst thing is what it does to the water. If you can't use your water, what are you going to do? People will leave. McCarthys are smart. They're selling and getting out now. They want the money, but they don't want to live with the results. If I could do that, I would. But my business, it's going to double, triple. So I'll do their dirty work, then I'll escape."

I only pretend to listen to my clients, because what I am really listening to is behind their voices. Twinges of pain and tenderness, points of resistance, that's what I'm looking for as I move across their bodies. Now I was going down his leg, deep-gliding with my thumbs, and I said, "Yeah, but it's hard to pick up your entire life, start over fresh someplace new."

"I'm ready. The human creature, it isn't a tree. We're a mobile animal."

There was resistance on his calf, and I was going into it with my thumbs. I could feel him wince. The light flickered as I murmured, "We'll see."

"And if drilling doesn't ruin this place, the ash borer will."

"Ash borer?"

"A small green insect moving its way north from Pennsylvania, eating the heartwood out of the ash trees."

"We have lots of ash."

"I'm sure it's most of what you have, and it's in Cattaraugus County now. Only a matter of time before it gets to Allegany."

"You're full of good news, aren't you?" But in truth, I was just making talk; my concern was with the real issues under my hands. I pulled the covers up to his neck and gently rocked him side to side like a baby. All the stiffness was gone.

Often I end the session at the client's head. I cradle it in my hands, my fingers working the suboccipital muscles where I believe Bruce's headaches originate. Then I focus on the face. This is my favorite part. It's rare when something hurts on the face, and my fingers knead and stroke like a mother comforting a worried child. *It's going to be all right. Everything will work out.* I put this message into my touch, and I tap, *All's well. All's well. You are a loved person.* My hands tapping, circling, pressing.

Bruce always leaves a hefty tip, and as I put the bills away in my drawer, I thought to myself, *No place is perfect*. Every rural location is under siege from something, and if you don't like it, then go to the city, where wildness is ruined already and lawns and parks are the only form of nature you get.

I call myself a massage *artist*. I know it's arrogant, but it's a thing I say only to myself. And I say it because every body I work on has an entirely different set of needs, and so I don't use the same routine on any two people. That would get boring. I did study all of that stuff about systems—the muscular, the nervous, the lymphatic, the skeletal—and I can identify everything under the skin at any location. Easy stuff, easy, but do I use it in my work? Rarely. It's not a matter of knowing systems; it's a matter of emptying that kind of knowledge out and watching. My hands are highly trained instruments with eyes of their own. They feel a problem, and they know what to do. The remedy is in my fingers, my elbows, my palms, my knuckles, my thumbs. It's in my complete relaxation and acceptance. If I'm tense and distracted, my client will feel it. So I stay focused. I bring warmth to ice, softness to stone. I find where my client has buried the shame and fear all of us carry around. I coax it away, and when it's gone I fan the ground with love. Hokey as it sounds, but after all, my name is Ramona, she of the wise hands. I watch, I feel, I imagine. That's why I can't have music.

In the early days, when I was fully and completely infatuated with Shep, I did him the same way. I listened and felt, and I think, I hope, that he, in his own blunt male way, did the same with me. Well, he did. I know he did. Because we developed this thing together. This life. He does the school; I do the garden, the chickens, and see about the bent and scarred bodies that come to me. It's worked out. The two kids, the farm, and then when the kids left home, we decided, or I decided, and he agreed, on goats. We had the barn, added the fencing.

I had fifteen minutes before my next client, so I went outside to the alley in back. There was a plastic chair out there; I think it's a smoking station for someone who cooks at the restaurant, and that's where I sit. I closed my eyes, bowed my head, and breathed the clean winter air.

It's startling to go from a male to a female, and in particular, to go from a

tall, ponderous man like Bruce to a small, nervous woman like Fern. She was in her early sixties, and her years of running a riding school kept her fit. The problems of her life went to her hips and lower back. Sometimes her piriformis was so tight I felt as though I were attempting to work metal. She liked the room cool, so I turned everything way down after Bruce left. She preferred me to work on her back. Some women feel undefended in the front, and Fern was one of them. I don't question it. And even on her back, I was careful to readjust the coverings after I exposed an arm or a leg. It's funny how protective people are. What is nakedness but a condition shared by us all? All variations are acceptable, and anyway, who's to say what we should look like unclothed?

"Wow," I said, "what's going on?" I was working on her upper back, gently pulling and shaking out each arm, pressing on the shoulder, but movement was inhibited. "Something happening in your life?" I added more gently.

"I thought I was doing a decent job hiding it." Her voice was wobbly with feeling.

I squirted more oil into my palms and moved up and down the canvas of her back as though I were spreading paint. Working quickly, loosening the fascia, moving heat into the muscles. I pulled the covers up to her neck and, lifting her thick grey hair to the side, I went back to her shoulders. I turned the sheet down at the very top. "I can listen," I offered. As I said, I'm not eager for talk, but touch releases emotions, and Fern is a woman who has a habit of holding them in.

She shot out a stream of breath. "It's my competitor. Darla Oswald. The only other person around here with horses. We've never been friends. I've tried, but it's a lost cause. She's just too ambitious to be interested. And aggressive as hell. She has more horses, more stables, a bigger riding ring, but I have more trails. Anyway, we compete for students. And she has too many horses. They're crowded and don't get enough exercise.

"So—but this is between you and me, okay? I don't want this spread around."

I said what I always say: "Anything I hear in this room stays here."

"Good. Well, the phone rings. This was last week. And there's this loud, aggressive voice. 'Fern Snyder,' she says. 'Darla Oswald. Bet you never expected to hear from me, did you? I have a proposition. Are you ready?'

"No 'How are you? How are your horses?' She's so brazen. Just goes straight to it. Like she's the President and has no time for a lowly person like me. So I took her down a notch. I said, 'Hello, Darla. How are you doing? Congratulations on those wins you took at State last September.'

"But Darla doesn't do conversation. 'I need to know something fast. Because I have to act soon. Life is biting my tail, so to speak. Fern...'

"'Yes,' I say. Now I'm a little nervous. What does this woman want with me?

"'I'm moving. Going back to where I grew up. Maybe just for a couple of years, and I can't take all of my horses. What I want to know is, would you be interested in looking them over and making me an offer for five or six?'

"'Moving? Whatever for? You're so established here.' We're competitors, but I like having someone else doing the same thing. It means it's not just me out there trying to convince people that riding and keeping horses is a great way of life. If she left, a full one-half of the equestrian scene would leave with her. That's a huge loss. So I'm feeling put out and a little angry.

"She says, 'Lookit, I want you to think it over and give me a call when you decide.'"

Women who do a lot of riding have unbelievable upper thighs. The muscles on the insides of their legs are larger than anyone's. But hers were rigid. I oiled up and did a fast hand-over-hand glide, pausing to shake the flesh. Then I moved to her feet. I pulled my stool around to the end of the table and picked one foot up, tucking the covers around her leg so nothing would be exposed, and began. There are fourteen thousand nerve endings in the feet, and I know how to stimulate every one of them. Fern has never said anything to me about her feet, which are thick and wide but flat. Like pancakes. No lift, which is why her hips have to carry it all.

All women, but Fern especially, need to have their toes worked. Toes are what roll our weight forward. And when there are burdens, toes are what hold them. Most women, at one time or another, have broken one. That's because when the burden is too heavy, the way too rough, it's a toe that gives out. So I give real time to a woman's toes. Each and every one of them.

"I had a hunch about something," Fern said. "So I took a chance. I said, 'Darla, when those leasing agents came to my place I ran them off. Sounds like you invited them in for a cup of coffee.'

"'What are you talking about?'

"'The Marcellus. The gas. The get-rich-quick guys who are running around this county leasing land.'

"'I'd never lease the mineral rights to my place. And I'd never sell it. I'm just closing it up for a couple of years, and going back to New Hampshire. If you must know, it's because my parents are getting old. So I'm suspending everything here for a little while, and doing things on a smaller scale at my parents' place, which is why I can't take all of the horses. And, Fern, you're not the only person I've approached. So think about it and get back to me, and I'll take the highest offer I get.'"

Fern has a very long big toe. It's a beautiful and noble creature, and it has room enough on the pad for me to get in and roll it around. I was working it with my thumbs when I said, "You're going to make an offer?"

"First of all, I don't believe a word of it. This is not a woman who drops everything to take care of elderly parents. You and I might do that, but not Darla. There is something else going on. Who knows? Something bigger and more important to her, because, in effect, her leaving for a year or two means I'll take over. She's willing to give me that opportunity because something's drawing her away that's worth it. What it is, I don't know. This is not a woman I'm friends with. Maybe she's after a man."

"So go check out her horses. Do it before you get cold feet." I said this while still on the toe, and something icy grabbed the back of my neck when she replied, "She'll be in New Hampshire this weekend. Otherwise, I would."

One of the best things about Andover is the town of Alfred, seven miles away. There's a college there and that's where the salon, with my back room, is located. There's also a couple of restaurants, and a small grocery that gets fresh fish and bread every Thursday. Helene, who runs it with her stepfather, William Swick, who owns the used bookstore next to it, drives up to Rochester very early every Thursday morning and brings it back. I go there every week, after my last massage, and buy whatever I need.

Sometimes I make a request and they'll have it for me on Thursday.

This Thursday, Helene had a bag of mussels I'd ordered and I bought a package of linguine, and a hunk of good grating cheese. The mussels were from Maine, picked off the rocks from the area around Blue Hill where we used to live. They were expensive, but it didn't matter. Shep was getting in late from Albany, and I wanted him to come home to a good dinner. I also bought red peppers and a small amount of fresh string beans. When I got to the register, Helene brought the mussels up front. "I have Shep's order. You could take that too, save a trip. Or maybe you have to come this way anyway."

"I don't know," I said carefully. "Refresh my memory."

"Let's see." She pulled a list out of a drawer and read two cupcakes, two ginger sodas, two apples, a package smoked salmon, smoked mozzarella, one box sesame crackers and a bag of spring lettuce. It's all bagged up in the cooler. I'll go get it."

I stopped her. "That's okay. He can come in the morning."

"Let him pay for it too," Helene added.

I recognized my husband in these choices. Trips, for him, were an opportunity to indulge in expensive snacks. I used to be a peanut butter sandwich, carrot stick sort of traveler, but Shep schooled me out of that. He'd pack a basket of goodies and then in the middle of the drive he'd pull off at a nice spot and make a picnic. I loved this about him.

"Where are you going?" Helene asked.

"New Hampshire," I said, feeling my cheeks heat up because it is impossible for me to lie.

"Nice. Well, have a good time. Drive safe. I hope the snow stays away. And hey, enjoy the mussels tonight. Sounds like a little celebration. Good for you!"

When I got home, I went out to check on the goat. I could hear him butting against the walls, and as I opened the door, he pushed his nose in the crack, but I slipped in and hooked it closed before he could get out.

The stall had a warm animal smell, and the little bit of hay I had put down was urine-soaked and marked with piles of little black balls. I added fresh hay to the floor and stuffed more in the basket I was using as a temporary hayrack. I also unhooked the water bucket and maneuvered my

way out the door without letting him escape. I scrubbed it out and filled it down at the hydrant. Carrying it back full, I made it in without getting any water down in my boots and locked it in place against the wall.

The goat was pulling tufts of hay out of the basket, eating some, but dropping more to the floor. I was surprised that on such a cold day the stall would feel as warm as it did and that his body would be even warmer. It felt so safe I didn't want to leave. So I squatted in the fresh hay next to him and leaned my head into his warm goaty flank.

"You need a name," I said. "What is your name?" He nuzzled against me, still chewing. "Dammit," I said. "I know your name. Mischief, that's what it is, isn't it?"

Back in the kitchen, I started dinner. I enjoy cooking for the simple reason that I like to eat good food. I'm a good cook because I take the time to imagine the dish before I make it. That's what I'd been doing up at the goat barn. I'd imagined the garlic-mussel sauce I was going to make for pasta. I'd pictured a bowl of spaghetti with a crown of opened mussels adorning it. Then I'd imagined a side dish of peppers, artichoke hearts, and string beans tossed with olive oil and vinegar.

First, I oiled the peppers and put them under the broiler. As they were heating, I cut up parsley, olives, garlic, and rinsed the beans. The counter was covered with colorful piles of chopped things. I set a pot of water on a high flame and put a fry pan on another burner. Soon things were sizzling and boiling and the kitchen windows were covered with steam.

Shep would be getting home soon, and I wanted to have everything ready. The flames leaped, the water jumped, the oil spat. I threw in the garlic and onions, grated pepper over them, and slammed on a lid. Then I poured the mussels into the steaming pot and slapped on another lid. Meanwhile, in the oven, the skin on the peppers was crisping. I placed them in a pot with a tight-fitting lid and let them sit for ten minutes. It's a trick I read. The steam makes them juicy.

That was when I heard a car grind up the driveway. But I didn't run to the window. Fifteen things were happening at one time, and though browned garlic is lovely, burnt garlic is trash. So I stirred and waited, and soon the back door popped open, and I could hear rustling in the mudroom as he removed his boots. The door to the kitchen opened, and I could hear him setting his briefcase on the floor, hanging his coat on the hook.

Usually, I say something, something welcoming as he comes through the hall, but this time I couldn't speak.

"Smells great!" he called.

I looked up when he came into view, and that was when it hit me. I have never been able to hide my feelings, and when I caught the scent of cold he brought into the room and saw the splotch of weather on his cheeks, I understood, like it was a new fact, that this man moved in a world I knew nothing about. There I am, locked up with naked bodies, while he's at a desk studying percentiles, regulations, budgets. I had always liked our differences. I couldn't do what he did, and he the same with me. If I asked him to rub my back, he did it, but not effectively, not well, because he had no feeling in his hands and no desire to confront pain. Now, with cold streaming away from his skin, he came to the stove and bent, slightly, to kiss me.

"Don't." My voice was husky with tears. "What's going on?" I whispered. "Why is Darla Oswald moving to New Hampshire?"

Shep has a wonderfully resonant voice, and when he laughs it is a spilling of notes that melts you. "What a strange question. I have no idea why or if she is. You seem to know. Is she? Boy, does it smell wonderful. What are you making?"

I should have known that a man who functions well in a political position is a man who knows how to keep secrets. Who knows how to work people. Not the way I do, but in the invisible, manipulative, behind-closed-doors bargaining that I've only seen in old movies where white-shirted men fill back rooms with smoke. "Who are you going to New Hampshire with?"

"Look," he said. "I've been driving for five hours. Let me sit down. Let me get something to drink. You can't imagine what this day has been like, and in two days I have to get in the car again."

"I'm sure you'll fortify yourself with delicious snacks. You and Darla."

"Yes, she's coming with me. She recommended me to the school, and she happened to be driving there this weekend, so it made sense. What is this? Are you accusing me of something?"

"I don't know. I don't know." I threw my hands up. Was I? The garlic was getting too brown. "I can't talk. I'll ruin this meal."

"What can I do to help?"

Such a simple, Shep-like question. Maybe it was all my imagination. "Just sit. Just sit and relax. Or set the table. Then relax." After all, he'd had a hard day; he'd been on the road. "Is it snowing?"

"Clear," he said, "but still cold. Supposed to drop to twenty below. Let's remember to keep the faucets dripping."

When it's cold like that, the kitchen is the only place in the house that feels cozy; the fire in the woodstove and the heat from cooking balances the assault of outside air. "Don't talk," I said. I was pulling the skin of the pepper away from the meat, and it was coming off in thin, wavery sheets. The mussels were done, and I threw the noodles into the fishy water and kept the flame high.

For some reason, he used our best china and silverware and lit a candle. It looked beautiful. The dishes on the counter, waiting for us, were beautiful too. But I felt as nervous as though it were a first date. I served the meal in shallow bowls and put a dish of grated cheese on the table.

The first forkful was so good. There was just the right amount of pepper and salt, and the mussels were fresh and sweet. But I had no appetite. "Is something going on?"

"Yes," he said. He put down his fork. "I told you I'm interviewing for a job. It's a job Darla put me in contact with because we work together on school issues and she went to this school as a young girl and she knows it well and is very active there as an alum."

"But are her parents really ill? She's really going back there to take care of them?"

"You know each other?" he asked.

"We met at the feed store," I said, remembering that I mustn't reveal anything a client tells me in the treatment room.

"I don't know her that way. We're not friends."

"But you're taking her to New Hampshire, not me. And you're

considering moving there without consulting me. I don't get it. I just don't get it. Are you and I finished?" There. My worst fear.

He looked up in surprise.

Shep carries authority even when he's sitting at the dinner table. Sometimes that authority makes me feel as though I were nothing but another one of his children, not only his two blood children, but his five hundred other children at the central school.

"Well, what am I supposed to think? I go into the grocery, and I find out you've ordered this romantic lunch for the road."

"It's food. I have to eat, don't I?"

"What's going on?" I said evenly.

"Look." He finally made eye contact. "I want to make this decision alone. I want to check it out alone. I don't want to have to consider all of your…"—he paused and finished more softly—"all of your stuff."

"What do you mean by that?"

"Your… requirements."

"Such as?"

"Your massage work; your desire for animals; for a private, rural place with no neighbors in view. I want to look this over for myself first. And then…"

I didn't let him finish. "So you'll make a decision for yourself, and then, at last, you'll ask my opinion. But by that time, it'll be too late."

"I'm tired. You know I have to leave this job. I have to go somewhere simple, where I'm not the enemy, where there's no taxpayer and no state government. It's killing me. I can't keep it up."

"You don't have a thing for Darla?"

Shep smiled. "Darla is an extremely seductive woman."

There it was.

But then his face broke open, and the man I remembered looked out. Oh yes, finally. Now why had he gone missing? It was the face I knew from our private moments, when the outside world disappeared and something boyish and grateful and entirely devoted took over. His eyes, the color of wet stones, glistened in the light. "But you have nothing to worry about, because you are, too."

The goat had been locked in his stall for three days. As I walked out to the barn, the snow crunched under my boots. The morning was cold, but he had a heavy winter coat, and he would know where home was now. When I opened the door, he came up and nuzzled against me, breath curling from his nostrils. I stomped on the water bucket to crack up the ice, filled it with fresh, put new hay in the basket, and came and went with the door open. He stayed indoors. He didn't even poke his head out to see the large fenced pasture where the chickens pecked even on that coldest day. When I finished my chores, I put a stone against the door so it would stay ajar and he could come and leave as he wished.

My requirements. Were they that difficult? The questions came and went as I rubbed and pressed into flesh. I couldn't pay attention to them as I worked, but when I broke for lunch, they came at me hard. I sat by myself in the village restaurant and thought about the way his job, his skills, organized my life. Did my job, my skills, organize his? What I knew, what I knew without question, was that every time he drove up the driveway, whether it was from a trip to Albany or a day at school, I couldn't wait to see him. I couldn't wait to tell my news and hear his, to put my arms around his body. Remembering that got me through the afternoon.

There was still some light by the time I got home. Darkness was in process, but I could see my way to the barn, and when I looked into Mischief's stall, I knew at once that it was empty. The pasture was empty too. The snow was slick under my feet, because the day had warmed up and then turned colder. I followed his footprints. He hadn't frolicked at all. There was only a single line. He'd come out of the barn and gone straight to the four-foot fence. He did it at a run, and on the first try, his body sailed over and he landed, hard, because the prints were deep, on the other side. Even in the low light, I could see his tracks crossing Darla's hayfield, climbing to the hills.

I knew what not to do.

But when I opened the door to the house, it was Bruce's voice I heard: *contiguous*. Of course. That's what was going on. It wasn't sex she was after—it was land. My Shep: principled, honorable, overwhelmed. He would be oblivious to her grand scheme. Shep needed a school without Albany; Darla needed contiguous land. If we were in New Hampshire, she could buy our acres.

I could imagine it all: truck traffic, well pads, containment pools. These hills and valleys: pools, pads, pollution. And then the word *love* added itself to the list. All the many possibilities. But where was the love in that vision? Shep would be in New Hampshire, educating the next kings of industry. And I would be where?

The moon rose over the tracks, glazing them with blue light, a chilly line stretching to somewhere else. That was not me. Oh no, that would not be me.

Three Rivers

Had Lana Leicester Smith been married a third time, she would have added that surname too. They were like degrees, each one providing a little extra gravitas, weighting her, connecting her, keeping her from lifting off on the next wind. Not that she was frail; it had to do with the perpetual flutterings of doubt and other havoc.

Having a husband had always helped, but now that she didn't, fear so paralyzed her it was difficult to leave her apartment. Only doctor appointments and the once-a-week visit to her therapist could override what had become a self-decreed house arrest. And she was lucky, her many windows made her feel like a participant; she could look down on the tops of the trees, she could see the Delaware river behind the Hyatt Hotel, and sometimes even the silhouette of Camden.

On this day, Lana was sitting in her bedroom, watching the comings and goings of cars and pedestrians when the phone rang. She picked it up greedily, but it was only Willow, her second husband's daughter. She knew the reason for the call. Tomorrow was the anniversary of her father's death, a date Willow still honored but Lana ignored. First, Willow inquired about Lana's health, but there wasn't anything new. Same old, same old, high blood pressure, high cholesterol, so she told Willow, "Not getting any younger, but not getting any older either!" They laughed, but for Lana it was true. She was going to live forever; she believed it just as she believed that she had never been a Jewish girl from Brooklyn.

Willow was an expert in Asian culture and like others in academia, she considered everything in life a chance for instruction, so in far greater detail than Lana would ever have bored Willow with, she described her realization, one of many she had offered Lana over the years: "I have decided not to mark Daddy's death this year because his spirit has passed on. I've meditated on it and consulted my teacher and what I've come to realize is that remembering his death, even lighting a candle, is to call his spirit back to the places and people it left long ago. That isn't beneficial for him or for me because his spirit has moved onward. It's selfish. I wanted to tell you," she said, "because I know you still have his ashes. You might want to consider having a private ceremony and letting them go."

Lana wondered why Willow kept track of who still had her father's remains.

"Not that you have to," Willow corrected. "That's your decision, I just thought I'd let you know."

Lana thanked her. She said she would think about it, told her to call the next time she came to Philadelphia. "Call in advance," she said, "because sometimes I'm busy." That was a lie, but she liked the illusion of a still well-connected older woman rushing from one obligation to another.

After hanging up the phone, Lana gave the top shelf in her bedroom a guilty glance. She pulled over the footstool and reached for the boxes she had put up there a long time ago. The better one was an antique of carved rosewood. It contained Leicester, her first husband. The lesser box was Smith, Willow's father, paper-covered cardboard, pretty to look at, but worthless. She dusted them off and placed them on the bureau in her foyer. Didn't a widow have the right to keep whatever she wanted, a woman alone, living on a finite income, having, as her financial advisor warned, to exercise care? Private ceremony! The truth was she had been planning to divorce Smith. But then he got sick.

Lana showered and chose her clothes carefully, a grey pants suit with a plum colored scarf that complimented her white hair and brown eyes. She put on sturdy walking shoes. She made sure she had enough twenties in her wallet and then, frightened of what she was about to do, called down to the front desk for a taxi. As she waited in the lobby, the two boxes in a canvas bag at her feet, she felt a wavering of courage. What if the driver took her to a lonely place, stole her purse, and drove away? It was too risky. But just as she stood to go back upstairs, a cab slipped into the slot at the front entrance. The driver, head wrapped in some kind of religious covering, looked into the lobby at Lana. Feeling marked by fate, she gripped her bag and walked towards him.

Of the two rivers in Philadelphia, the Schuykill, the river of Eakins, skull racing, and cherry blossoms, was the better one. She explained to the back of the driver's head wrapping (was he unable to turn around because he had slept in the wrong position, like she sometimes did, and had a crick in the neck?) that he was to wait right there in the parking lot below the art museum, but he only nodded and in a soft, lilting accent mumbled, "yes, ma'am." Praying he understood English, Lana set forth, watching for uneven footing, turning around as often as she dared to make sure the cab was still there. It was a beautiful day in April, just before the azaleas would flower, just before the park would explode into brilliant color.

When she reached the river she found a spot screened by a budding tree where there was a flat, fairly level stone she could stand on. She held the box aloft, turned it over, and removed the lid. The hard, pebbly bits of bone, all that was left of the modest man she had admired, but found impossible to live with, dribbled into the beautifully clear water. Ten years ago those bones had worn the flesh of a person she had considered her friend, even after the break-up, though as a friend, husband number one still drove her crazy. She said a little goodbye: "Gordon. Sweetheart. I miss you terribly. Things are fine here. I hope they're fine where you are." Then she walked back, slowly, carefully, waving to the driver every few steps so he wouldn't leave her.

The next stop was the lesser river, the river of transportation, industry, and secret chemical dumps. She told the driver to take her to the World War Two submarine anchored just south of the Towers and instructed him to park as close as he could get. Feeling his eyes on her back, Lana walked over the expressway towards the water. After the Towers had been built, the neighborhood had been cleaned up, but there was no hiding the roar of millions of cars under her feet. A tanker chugged downriver, but the Delaware was so big, so wide, there were no ripples, not even any sloshing against the pier. She held the box containing Willow's father over the water. Before dying, husband number two had let go of his bowels all over her bathroom and that final gesture in a long and boring illness still felt like a commentary on her: *I shit on you and your ridiculous lies!*

"Bye, bye!" she cried as the chalky chips sank into the sludge. Then she returned, slowly, carefully, waving to the driver the whole time, but he didn't once bother to wave back. Even so, she tipped him well.

When Lana closed the door to her apartment she noticed that already her rooms felt lighter, happier. Maybe Willow was right. Everyone needed to move onwards.

"I'm glad you did that," said Barbara Cohen.

Lana was wrapped in the dull light that squeezed through slatted blinds, molded into the hard modernistic chair the therapist provided for clients, while she lounged in an old-fashioned tufted recliner. "It was cleansing," Lana said, although it hadn't felt cleansing at all. It had simply been a duty, assigned by Willow, that she had performed. She said musingly, "I want to be married again."

"Why?" Barbara asked and Lana thought about how to answer.

"If there was a man in my life, I would feel protected."

"But haven't you told me that you're done with men?"

"I can still want one around, can't I? It would be comforting."

"You're the one who told me you loved the simplicity of your life without them. You said men were too complicated."

"But they're also convenient. Look, I miss intimacy. We might as well be clear about that."

Barbara believed sex was the root cause of all neurosis and so every once in awhile, Lana delivered what she hoped would be a significant confession.

"I miss touching, whispers, the goodnight kiss. I miss the company of a man, that solid other person who shares a space." She was thinking that a husband was like a best friend you could cuddle with when she remembered Viagra. Who wanted an old man with the erection of a twenty year old? The whole notion of collapsed, dessicated people having intercourse disturbed her because the truth was... What was the truth? Well, she hesitated to name it, because once you said a thing, there it was, out there, and Barbara, who was relentless and smart, would pin it to her record. But the truth, the secret truth, was that a man who couldn't get it up was her preference. Saying it out loud would invite discussions she wasn't willing to engage in, so she reached for something more general. "Sex scares me." There. That was an actual true statement.

Barbara seized it immediately. "Back to your core issue," she said in a careful and professional tone. "Why does sex cause fear?"

"Everything causes fear," Lana said, falling back on a statement she'd made many times before. But the clock on Barbara's desk chimed softly. Time had run out so they'd begin with sex and fear at the next session.

Thursday was her weekly consultation with her nutrition counselor. That morning, Lana checked the living room to determine if it was still a beautiful place. Her plants and furniture were arranged in a pleasing manner and the Chinese scroll, hanging over the antique table, was bathed in sunlight from the window. The scroll was from the Qing dynasty, very old, a mountain scene painted in faded inks, a river meandering between jagged cliffs. It was such a beautiful object, she wondered sometimes if the scroll were the real reason she'd married Willow's father. It was the scroll she'd fallen in love with. The small river, beginning in the mountains, spilling down through the cliffs, was like a child moving farther and farther from the place she was born. That river was as determined to escape its beginnings as she had been. She had left the big dining room, the Sunday meals, the beef tongue sitting at the center of a table where the cousins pinched and poked each other while the aunts and uncles examined the lives of everyone in the family: who was more deserving, more faithful, more willing to suffer the hatreds and discriminations of the chosen people. When she was eighteen she'd moved to Philadelphia and never went back. So the river winding through the mountains belonged on her wall, in her living room, and the man who came with the scroll was a bonus. At least until he lost all of his money and took up with another female. His disease was another trial, but unlike pennilessness or philandering, it was, thank the Buddha, fatal.

Lana made the preparations. She brewed imported green tea in an earthenware pot and set out an assortment of Japanesey snacks, all from the one natural foods store that made deliveries. When everything was ready, her phone rang, the desk clerk announcing her visitor, and soon Marlene Osaka was seated across from her. On the floor, she'd parked a case filled with various supplements, all of them costly, all of them with names that eluded meaning: CoQ10, Essential Seven, 5 HTP.

"Very good," Marlene was saying. "Your skin has improved tremendously. Have you noticed? It's tighter, more alive."

"Yes," Lana agreed, stirring so much enthusiasm into her voice she herself was convinced. "It's so much smoother."

"Now, can you remove your glasses? For just a moment?"

Lana stared trustingly into milky space.

"Yes, just as I thought." Marlene's finger came out of the mist and pointed to the grey, crinkly bags under her eyes. "Too much refined flour. That's the cause."

"Oh dear," Lana said, but really, weren't eye bags the least of it? Her entire physical statement was wrong. Large breasts, frizzy hair, eager, thrusting nose...nothing was subtle.

"Your body is storing too many toxins. All the heavy metals from city living, they get sent to the liver, which is why you're taking liver cleanse, but the overflow goes into these membranes under your eyes. That's why they're puffy. These bags are what greet every person you look at, and luckily, I have a specially formulated ocular toxin release, developed for this very problem, and I'm going to prescribe a heavy dose for the first few weeks till we see a diminishment. Now, I'll just take a little measurement," she said, brandishing her tool.

Marlene had a wand for measuring things that could not be measured. It was the size of a travel tooth brush with a little button that made a very small ruler pop out. She had measured Lana's belly sag, her upper arm sag, her shoulder hump, and now she leaned forward and measured the bags under her eyes. As she did so, she made tiny marks in her book with a mechanical pencil and then she bent down to rummage in her satchel, glossy hair curtaining her movements.

Lana felt such longing she said, apropos to nothing, "I need to do something about this." She indicated her own hair. "It's so dry and lifeless. What do you use in yours?" If only she could *be* Marlene Osaka.

"Two capfuls of this liquid in one cup of water twice a day and I promise we'll see results." Marlene added numbers to her bill and set a white bottle on the table.

"My hair," Lana reminded her, touching the impossible fluff that surrounded the face she had despaired over for so many years. She was a musk ox from the Museum of Natural History, eons old, reconstructed with moldering fur.

Very gently, Marlene touched her chin and turning her face towards her, her marvelous fingers resting for just a second on Lana's cheek, she fluffed out Lana's curls. "Please, show me your nails."

Lana held out her hands and Marlene peered down.

"Ah," she said.

"What?"

"Ridges. That means a lack of calcium. Please, would you open your mouth?"

"Ah," Marlene said again, peering into her mouth. "After the toxic release, we'll need to supplement with a formula that's aimed specifically at hair, teeth, and nails. A calcium, magnesium boost fortified with silica from an ancient herb called horsetail."

"That sounds good."

"It will help," Marlene said, sipping her tea, holding the cup in her long-fingered goddess hand. Lana had seen hands like it in the galleries of Eastern Art at the Philadelphia museum. "But I have to wait until after the release?"

"It would be best," Marlene said.

"Will you remember?"

"Of course," she said. "I've made a note of it in my book and I will make a note on your weekly chart." Lana watched as the instructions were put in both places, and then she saw how, with a secret movement, a barely perceptible tilt of her head, Marlene glanced at her watch. But Lana jumped in before she could make any sounds about leaving, and cried out, "You are so wonderful! I am so grateful for all of your help." Without a pause, without waiting for a reply, she opened her checkbook and went on in a gay, friendly tone. "I always benefit so very much. What do I owe you?"

Marlene showed her the total and then ripped off a copy of the bill and Lana wrote a check for one hundred over the amount as she always did and, on the memo line scrawled, *for you*. She kept a mental tally of these gifts, and by now, figured it came to a thousand dollars. She took Marlene's melon colored jacket out of her closet and held it open as first one and then another creamy arm slid into the silken sleeves.

"It's always a treat to spend an afternoon in your beautiful apartment. I so enjoy looking at all of your pretty things." Marlene leaned close and pecked Lana's cheek with closed lips.

"Love you," Lana called.

In the middle of the night a cat yowled in the parking lot. An emergency vehicle screamed down a nearby street. People laughed below her windows, and in the artificial light squeezing through the blinds Lana saw her mother Sylvia sitting in her room like an invited guest, accusing her. But of what, she wanted to say. Of what? Not wanting to stick around and be a good Jew?

At age fifty-seven Sylvia had died from a massive heart attack. Now, the same thing was happening to her at seventy-nine. She felt heavy. There was something heavy sitting on her chest, suffocating her, and now with the husbands in the rivers, there was no one. She turned on her bedside lamp, put on her glasses. That was better; everything came into focus. Could she speak?

Oh my god, she couldn't breathe, she couldn't speak! It *was* a heart attack! She was having a heart attack! She was dying! Exactly! There was numbness! Numbness in her upper arms! Constriction at her throat! A heavy weight on her body, oh my god, oh my god, who to call? Who could she call at two fifteen in the morning?

The last number she'd called on her phone. Of course! What could be easier? She stared at the buttons, searching for redial. Then she remembered, the last call had been to Marlene. Could the new ocular rinse cause diarrhea? But Marlene hadn't answered and she had left a long and friendly message, acknowledging all of the silly things one had to acknowledge with modern women, that she knew how busy she was, how very little time she had, that she was willing to wait, but the diarrhea was really a problem. Should she continue to take the formula or should she stop? Now, she lifted the phone to her face, because even with her glasses, her vision was wavy. A heart attack affected the entire body, so no wonder her vision was wavy. Redial! Redial! Where was the button? As she stabbed it with her finger, she thought about how she would present herself.

"Yes?"

"This is Lana. Lana Leicester? Lana Leicester Smith? At the Towers?

"Yes, can I help you…"

"I left you a message. Could diarrhea be an effect of the ocular rinse?" As she said these words she realized that she could talk and, therefore breathe, and she knew, in a flash, that it wasn't a heart attack at all, merely a moment of panic. "I'm sorry Marlene. It's so late. Forgive me. But I woke up and I'm having a panic attack. I'm worried about my heart. I was scared, so I pushed redial. I'm so sorry, but it's hard to be alone and I was wondering if it was at all possible. Are you up? It sounds like you're up. It's my heart. My mother, you see…." But her mother had rejected her.

"You should call 911."

"This is so awful, I'm so embarrassed. Who calls at this ridiculous late hour?" She laughed, just to show she saw the humor of it.

"You should call 911."

"There wouldn't be traffic. You said you lived just on the other side. I just…."

"You should call 911 if you think you're having a heart attack."

"I'm scared," Lana bleated.

"Call a friend or a family member."

"Please…"

"I can't talk now; I will see you at our next scheduled appointment."

"Oh my god," she wailed. "Oh my god!" But then she stopped, remembering the checks. It had to be a thousand dollars. Wasn't it? How many hundreds had there been? "No, I don't think so!" she announced, her heart beating a war dance. She would show this little snip, this little twat. "I'm quitting! And I will never recommend you or any of those boutique products you sell for outrageous prices to any of the people I know. No one, nothing, never!" She stabbed the End button.

Then she walked to her kitchen. Did she really walk to her kitchen? Was everything working? Arms, legs, brain? She opened the cabinet and took out all eight Nature's Wisdom products. She dropped them in a grocery bag and headed towards her door. Then she paused. Should she put a coat on over her nightgown? Slip shoes onto her feet? No, she should not. She should simply do it. She should not hesitate. She should not overthink the first spontaneous act of her life. So, with a burst of strength, she flung her door open and marched into the hallway. She *did* hear it close behind her, but paid no attention. She padded past all of the other doors, where everyone else was sleeping the sweet restorative sleep of mild people. Nighttime was theatre for the fierce! Feet on the carpet, eyes on the textured wall, she flung open the small door next to the elevators, pulled down the metal cover, and dropped, one by one, each Nature's Wisdom bottle into the trash chute. They shot through the metal sleeve, journeying from the sixteenth floor to the dumpster in the sub basement.

At the next session with Barbara C., Lana had nothing to say about sex and fear, but she feigned interest and waited until the game was in full play. Then, when she had center stage, she wondered timidly if Barbara might be able to prescribe something to help her sleep. Barbara asked why and Lana said, "Because if a siren goes off I wake up and think I'm having a heart attack. I want something that will make me sleep through sirens and cat fights and drunk teenagers laughing in the parking lot."

Barbara suggested she invest in a white noise machine. Or simply set up a fan. Lana ignored these remarks and announced, "You will be pleased to hear I have expressed myself in a bold manner."

"Really?"

But Lana, catching the half-lidded glance, didn't answer.

So Barbara rephrased, gave it more conviction: "Wonderful! I'm so anxious to *hear*!"

"Anger," Lana said, amazed that the emotion that had eluded her for her entire life didn't possess a more elaborate sound. "For once, I could feel it." Now there was a flicker of interest in Barbara's eyes, so she described, moment by moment, the events of that night. She reported the excitement of walking down the hallway in her nightgown, ended with the last Nature's Wisdom bottle hurtling down the chute. "And then," she added, as though it hardly mattered, "I couldn't get back in. I had to wait until 6:00 a.m. when the parking attendants arrived."

"So what did you do?" Barbara asked, and for once she seemed involved. After all, anyone could get locked out of her apartment. And if Barbara dumped her trash at two in the morning wearing only a nightgown... well, even a doctor with a lot of fancy degrees could be embarrassed.

"I sat there. I had nothing on, literally, except for a thin, an absolutely nothing little see-through thing." Lana paused to gather herself. "Those boys who work in the sub-basement. They're youngsters! Well, the night attendant, he must have been asleep because it wasn't until 6:00 a.m. Let me tell you, they had a fright the next morning. *Help me! Help me on the sixteenth floor!* A voice in the corner by the dumpster. And when they came up, which they did, all three of them, well, I don't have to tell you, everything was exposed." Lana indicated the generous slope of her chest. "But they were very gentlemanly. Didn't stare. Not one bit."

When Lana saw that the pad in Barbara's lap, where she continuously took notes was blank, she was flooded with a feeling of success. Here it was. After so many years, and so many checks written to Dr. Barbara Cohen, the client/therapist relationship had dissolved. For the first time, they were simply two women, two equals, two human creatures picturing a situation. She felt the glow of companionship and wondered if that were all she had ever really wanted. Just that. Not a cure, not a change.

The Exit Coach

1.

In the west nineties, where the streets sloped down to Riverside Drive, the apartment buildings, following the incline, seemed as geologic as rock face along a canyon wall. To Marilyn, who had grown up there, it was a feeling common to that part of the Upper West Side, something about history, and how it wouldn't let go, or the power of the river, resting below them, or she didn't know what, maybe the actual rocks underneath the buildings. Maybe the rocks were so massive they made a whole other place, rooms and tunnels below them that nobody knew anything about, but standing next to such ancient foundations, such ordered wildness, Marilyn felt small and even silly. And to be trapped against the wall in her graduation gown, while shoppers and nannies and all the other people walked by in ordinary clothes, was embarrassing. She wanted the photo session to end, but there was no rushing Cleopatra.

"Okay, honey girl, keep still. This last one's for the album."

Her mother disappeared behind the camera once again and there was the same squishy sound as the Polaroid fixed another pose for all of time. Cleopatra pulled the paper out, shook it to make the chemicals dry faster, and they watched together as Marilyn's indistinct figure swam into clarity against the granite blocks of the building. "My graduate," Cleopatra announced, holding the photo at arms length to see it better and then sliding it into her bag to show her friends at work. Then her mother walked east to go to her job and Marilyn walked south to go to the ceremony she was relieved her mother would have to miss.

Because even with the diversity of the public school, Cleopatra would have been a question mark. She was always a question mark. Her large, heavy presence, ferocious black-lined eyes, glistening pink curls, were incomprehensible. She obeyed no categories: too unlikely to be a mother, too unlikely to be a grandmother, and too dramatic for all things, even if she were wearing her brown transit worker uniform.

After the ceremony, when clusters of family swallowed the other graduates, Marilyn returned her rented garb to the front office and slipped away in the pale and modest dress she had worn underneath the gown. Her plan for the rest of the afternoon was to find a way to become another person, a person with a different identity, someone not named after the sexiest woman of modern times.

And so, at three o'clock exactly (she knew because church bells were chiming), she pulled open the glass door of a company called Silver Linings. The woman at the desk, putting her hand over the mouthpiece of the phone, indicated a row of chairs. As Marilyn waited, the platitudes from the morning, uttered in an auditorium buzzing with perfume and heat and babies' cries, swelled into actual fact: *West Side graduates don't shirk hard work or challenges. West Side graduates seize opportunity when it comes their way. West Side graduates are known for their willingness to learn and their uncompromising moral ethic. They are motivated and fearless and that's why, in this great hall, friends and family have come to celebrate the achievements of the class of 1977 and usher them into the temples of continuing education that await them. And one of those temples, my friends, is life itself. Life in all of its boldness and cunning, its temptations and false rewards. West Side graduates are prepared for life's skirmishes, large and small.* Had she been there, Cleo would have whispered loudly, what a lot of horsecrap!

"You're quite a bit younger than our average applicant," the woman said. "This isn't the kind of job that appeals to someone your age, but maybe you've already had experience? A grandmother, grandfather?" She looked up. "No?" Her eyes seemed to be stuck on the blank lines in the portion of the application labeled Prior Job Experience and as Marilyn watched her, she knew the heroic words from the morning's address *were* horsecrap.

"There are people out there, I'm not saying you're one of them, but there are lots of people who think this is easy work. That's not true. It takes a great deal of patience, not to mention a mature attitude for things like…Well, to be frank, vomit, sickness, diapers. If that's disgusting, this is not the job for you. But there are also benefits. That's why we call ourselves Silver Linings. Because despite all the ugliness, and let me be specific, the ugliness of bodily fluids, of dementia, all of which is part of the care of the elderly, there's a chance for deep and lasting friendship."

Until they croak, Cleo would sneer.

The interviewer tapped her pen on the desktop, leaned back in her chair, and said, "I'm a little dubious. But maybe you can tell me why you think you'd be good at this?"

"I don't know," Marilyn began. "I'm patient. I'm really quiet. And I like older people. I like history. I think I'm unusual that way. I just graduated high school and I figure the only other thing that's open to me probably is a waitress. But I'd rather do this. I mean, I really would like to have a job like this."

"I see. Have you ever, at any time, for any reason, been apprehended by enforcement personnel?"

"Enforcement personnel?" She blanked. "No, I don't think so."

"What I'm asking is, do you have a police record? We check all of our applicants but I like to ask first because that makes my job easier."

Marilyn smiled at the absurdity of such a mild, boring person like herself being arrested. "Oh! No, no, not at all. I'm not adventurous. I sort of, I don't know, I guess I crave stability. I don't like risk or change. I like things to be peaceful. It's kind of hard graduating for that reason, not having something to go to next. It's really big out there if you know what I mean. If you don't have something to go to," she finished lamely.

As soon as she walked into their apartment, Marilyn saw the pad of paper with Silver Linings and a phone number. The TV laughed. She glanced into the living room where smoke curled into the air from a cigarette burning by itself in an ashtray. An arm extended from a body hidden by the BarcaLounger; slender fingers lifted the cigarette, put it down. The arm came out again, returned a wine glass.

"Cleo? When did they call?"

There was a pause while her mother muted the sound. "Around four."

"Did they say anything?"

"Why would they say anything? I could be anyone. They're not going to tell your business to anyone but you. What's it about? Who are these people? Listen, I hope you're not going around laying yourself open for all kinds of monkey business. They take advantage of people like you. Believe me. You got to be sharp. And don't give out our number like that."

"How am I supposed to get a job then?"

The BarcaLounger swiveled around and a mass of pink regarded her. "What kind of name is Silver Linings? Who are they? My God, it sounds like a whore house."

"It's an agency that sends aides into old people's homes to take care of them. It's better than minimum wage and I think it would be nice. You cook and clean up and help them do laundry. You go to the doctor with them. Nothing medical. You just…"

"What you do, sweetheart, is wipe shit from their ass. That's what that's about. You empty commodes and put on diapers. That's no kind of job."

"I think I would like it. There's no pressure like you would have in a restaurant."

"But honey sweetheart, she didn't say Marilyn. She said something else, some other name, Angel or Abigail. Some A sound. Though it *was* Prett. I heard the Prett." Cleopatra tossed her head and the mass of curls she formed with the hair dryer every morning bounced in the wind of her movement. She never drank hard liquor or beer, only rosé, and now she drained the glass to punctuate her words. Then she pulled a Kleenex from the bosom of her slip and drew the pink bathrobe, as fluffy as ostrich feathers, around her plump body. "She musta been calling someone else. Some other Prett because I heard distinctly that it wasn't Marilyn."

Marilyn dragged one of the chairs over from the table and positioned it in front of her mother. "I'm Ava," she said, sitting down and looking at her mother in the habitual way that bypassed the actual and viewed instead an abstract. She looked at the shape of a mother, not the real form.

"Yes! That was it. Exactly. Who is Ava Prett?"

"I'm Ava Prett."

"Well, pray tell," she oozed, her voice low and unctuous, the tone she used with tourists who hadn't heard what she said the first time and her superiors at the bus company when they failed to notice that she had already told them everything they needed to know.

"I went to City Hall and changed my name. It took a month and that's who I am now."

"So you lied about your age."

"No, eighteen was all they wanted. Once you're eighteen, you can."

"Something so terrible about the name I gave you?"

"I don't like it."

"How could you not like your own name?"

"I don't like who you named me for."

"The world's most alluring woman? Like Cleopatra, only I couldn't name you Cleopatra because I wouldn't do that to you. It's not good for people in the same family to have the same name."

"She killed herself, Mom. She was a drug addict. She was so unhappy."

"What am I, a mind reader? That all came later. The troubles, the suicide. When you were born she was beautiful, carefree, and happy. Very happy. Bending over that subway grate? The skirt billowing? Oh God, happy go lucky!"

"I know, I know, you've told me. But I can't say it without thinking of her and it's sad, it's really sad. So now I'm Ava."

Cleopatra put the cigarette to her lips and drew in a long, indulgent rope of smoke that she exhaled slowly. Then she lifted her glass and drained it. She stood up, slipped her feet into pink pom-pom toed satin slippers and padded into the kitchen. The light went on.

"You changed *your* name when you were young. So what's the difference?"

"It's a world of difference. And if you can't see it, I'm not going to explain. Besides, it's done."

"You know, some people might think Esther is a better name than Cleopatra."

"Some." The water ran into the sink, was shut off. "But not me."

She came back, drying a wine glass with a kitchen towel. "Okay, so who are you now?"

"Ava."

She poured rosé into both glasses and handed one to her daughter.

Cleopatra raised hers. "We'll have a toast. To celebrate a new person, graduated from high school, entering the impossible world. May Ava Prett do more in her life than wipe shit from old people's backsides."

2.

"You behave yourself. And don't you try going to the john. Use the commode when you're alone. And if I was you, and thank the Good Lord I'm not a nasty old Jew, put away that wallet. Hide it, you hear? And not just in the cabinet. Some place nobody would think of. The teapot let's say. You be good now and I'll see you next week."

Maxi Bruder, her short, thick body wrapped in the black clothing of a woman in perpetual mourning, her stumpy legs encased in compression hosiery, had been his housekeeper for thirty years, but the game of insults had been going on for only a few months.

"Not if I can help it you old, ugly Kraut. Give my regards to the bookie."

"He's busy. Too busy for the old wife. Has too many girlfriends." But she smiled her bitter smile and he wondered if maybe the girlfriends she was talking about were horses. Maxi draped her raincoat over her arm and picked up the satchel that contained not only her pocketbook and house slippers, but a China figurine that, until that afternoon, had stood on the crowded shelves in the dining room.

It was a troubadour, one of thirty from his dead wife's collection. Modeled out of porcelain and painted by hand, it was authentic Meissen porcelain, crafted near Dresden where the Bruders, Mr. and Mrs., had been born. He was leaving the entire collection to her in his will, but Harvey wondered if maybe it would be kinder just to give them to her now while he was still alive. Then she wouldn't feel obliged to steal. He hated the goddamn things anyway.

When the door shut behind her, he wheeled himself into the music room and sat there for some moments enjoying the solitude. His apartment was on the top floor at the front of a building facing Central Park and the sunshine that spilled through the windows felt celestial. It was his bird heaven, a tree-top palace that leaned into clouds and jet trails, schmoozing with God and all his attendant saints and angels. Peace. A place to wait for death, though death certainly was taking its time. Wheelchair bound, but clear of mind, he wanted to take care of a few things before his name was called, his thread was cut, or the kindly mule kicked his particular bucket.

Or that's what he told himself. Really, he was only existing. Only breathing, shitting, thinking, admiring the view, and listening, listening with all his senses.

With the help of his son, of course, who had lowered the stereo so Harvey could get to it from the chair. Ruben had also installed handles, in the kitchen and bath, the two rooms too narrow for a chair with big wheels.

People with ulterior motives (Maxi, for instance) tried to make him dependent, but he was perfectly able to take care of himself and he preferred it that way because when someone else was in the apartment, they cluttered it with worries and obsessions and kept him tethered. Alone, he soared in the stillness of space and light and gained the purity of sounds he had always been after.

The tape that was on the player happened to be the one he wanted to hear; he pushed the "on" button and the room filled with the tune he craved: the Duke on piano, Grapelli on violin. But the first piece hadn't even ended when a question tiptoed into his consciousness. Why did she tell him to hide his things?

The answer came that evening when he picked up the phone.

"Daddy? How're you feeling? How's that cold? Maxi said you had a cold."

"Oh, that's nothing, just a few sniffles. Maxi exaggerates."

"You should take something for it. You don't want it to turn into pneumonia. Please take something for it. I'll have the drugstore send up something to make you sleep better. Some Nyquil, okay?"

"It's fine. I sleep fine. There's no need."

"I would feel so much better if I knew you had it. Just in case. Know what I mean? Just in case."

"I don't need it," he said. "How's John? How're the children?"

"Everyone's fine. Everyone sends their love."

"Well, everything's all right here. I'm healthy. No need to worry."

There was a pause. "Just a minute," she said.

He could hear her put the receiver down, whisper to someone, and then pick it up again, but she hadn't made a sound. Then cautiously, in a new tone, "Daddy?"

"Jennifer my love." What he had always called her.

"Don't be angry with me. Let's just try it first, okay? Someone is going to come, starting tomorrow for four hours just to help, just to make things easier for you, okay? It's a very good agency. No one they send has a criminal record. Everyone is screened, very carefully, and if for some reason you don't like this person you can ask for someone else."

He snorted in disgust.

"Wait…. don't say anything. Let me just tell you how I feel, okay? It's really hard." Her voice cracked. "You don't know. But sometimes at night I lie in bed just thinking about you all alone. What if you fell? You could starve to death."

She had been like this as a child. He once told Alice that he regretted telling Jennifer how long they had tried for a child. It was almost as though she had absorbed into her being all the vulnerabilities of those eggs as they attempted the heroic journey. Alice used to sit with Jennifer on the nights she couldn't sleep, stroking her forehead, singing the great old songs, but softly, turning them into lullabies.

"Listen, my love, I'm fine. When you can't sleep, just put on one of your mother's recordings. That'll work. It'll work better than saddling me with someone I don't want and don't need. Let's not do this. Call them tomorrow and cancel it."

"You're sure?"

"I'm sure."

"It's just me?"

"That's all it is. Trust me."

"Oh Daddy, it would be so much easier if I lived closer. Listen, don't you think you could try it, just for a few days? You might be surprised."

"Call tomorrow, Jennifer. Cancel the person."

3.

At nine a.m. when the doorman rang and said, "You have a visitor Mr. Abram," he knew that Jennifer hadn't canceled. And now the whole tiresome business would begin. Two weeks later, if it lasted even that long, he would decide that his privacy was more important, and feeling like an ass, he would fire the overburdened, underpaid Caribbean, Vietnamese, Puerto Rican woman who had spent an hour on public transportation and then with poor language skills and a volatile mixture of hates and fears, tried her absolute best to understand his needs.

A knock on the door came next. Soft, but he heard it. He had lived by his hearing all of his life and in old age was still blessed with it. It was his legs that had given out.

"It's open," he called, wheeling himself into the foyer, preparing to meet the enemy.

But the person who stepped onto the parquet Maxi kept so slick with wax he joked that she was trying to kill his visitors, promptly fell on her backside and a pair of ridiculously impractical shoes flew off her feet. "Oh! Oh gosh, I'm sorry!"

"Well, the first thing is that you'll need sneakers for my floors. Those shoes will kill you." He couldn't see her face yet, but he followed the motions as a swirl of legs and arms and some kind of navy outfit (my God, did they come now in uniform?) righted herself. "And you are?" Maybe it was a new person from the drugstore who didn't know deliveries went to the front desk.

"Ava Prett from Silver Linings, sir. Are you Mr. Harvey Abram?"

"Well, I used to be and unless something alien has claimed me, and of course it has, because that's what old age is, but it hasn't claimed all of me, not just yet, I still am. At your service." He actually (oh you fool, you seductive idiot) bowed his head.

She laughed.

At least Ava Prett had a sense of humor.

"Shoes go by the door, you can be barefoot, it will be safer, and belongings in the closet." But he noticed she had brought nothing with her. "Put the kettle on the stove, you'll find teabags and cups in the cupboard, and we'll have tea in the living room and a little chat."

He situated himself at the head of the table so he could see her as soon as she came through the door, and while he listened to preparations he asked himself what he was going to do. This was a girl, not a woman. A girl was not fair, prepared as he was to face another Maxi Bruder, armed with decrees and opinions, right ways and wrong ways, and most annoying, the belief that he was helpless. But this was a human person totally unformed. How could he turn her away? What if she could sing? Yes, what if she could sing?

She was not beautiful. Thank God for that. But as she brought the tray in, good, he'd forgotten to mention the tray, she looked at him. She smiled. What a smile! "You're strong," he said out loud, but only for himself. But she heard it and replied, setting a cup in front of him, a teapot, another cup for her, "Not really. Some girls at my school did weights, but I didn't."

"Even so, you are a strong person. You are full of beginnings."

She stirred sugar into her tea. For a moment, it looked like she might say something, but then she didn't. And then she said, "It's my first job."

"Your first job ever or for this agency?"

"Ever. I graduated high school two days ago."

"Do you play an instrument?"

"No, I wanted to, but in the end I didn't."

"Which instrument?"

"Clarinet."

No hesitation, he noticed. "I'll play you some Benny Goodman. Ever hear of him?"

"No, but thank you."

"The greatest clarinet player ever lived. Are you Jewish by any chance?"

"No, or at least my mother never told me."

"That's okay, doesn't matter. Benny Goodman was Jewish, that's why I asked. Ever do any singing?"

She giggled. "Star Spangled Banner? Not really, no."

He started it. "Oh say can you see, by the dawn's early light. What so proudly we hail . . ."

She didn't join in. Leave it alone, his better, less greedy self instructed. Don't make her nervous. "That's okay. It's a terrible song. We'll get to the singing part of things later."

"I thought I was supposed to do dishes, serve food, stuff like that."

"Sure, sure. All of that. That would be good. I was just wondering, on the off chance, you know. Mining for talent. That's what I do. What I did, rather, and it's hard to stop a thing when you've been doing it for so many years. It was how I met my wife. Alice Long, ever hear of her? Probably not, you're too young. She's been gone fifteen years now, but once she came through that door just like you did. Another apartment of course. And I was just starting out then. And really, I was only a couple of years older than her. Why, when I first met Alice Long I hardly had a list at all. A kid, wet behind the ears. But that's what she was too. So I said, 'Sing me something.'"

What shall I sing? she asked. That clear, bell-like voice.

Anything, I don't care.

"You see, I was pretending it didn't much matter because I wanted to see what she would choose. Well, she sang 'Evenin', the greatest blues song in the world. That was first of all what impressed me. But second was the authority of her voice. The wisdom. She delivered that song as though she had lived in it and her tone, it was syrup. Thick, sticky, endlessly sweet. Oh God, what a woman. Though a girl then, not much older than you."

"Did she fall on the floor too?"

He laughed. "Very good." Well, it was clear that Ava had timing, maybe even some humor. Yes, something was there. "Look at me."

She looked up. White oval face, a long nose. It was a strong, prominent nose, brown eyes, very short bangs and dark hair absolutely straight. Like an Egyptian. There was some kind of authority about her too, because she held his gaze, didn't blink, didn't even look like she *wanted* to turn away. "I see you," he said.

And she said, very simply, "I see you too."

"So listen: Let me tell you something. What I need help with, there's not much. We'll make it up as we go along. Can you cook?"

"Yes," she said.

But he spied uncertainty. She was only being brave. "You can't cook worth beans."

"I can learn. I'm sure I can do it."

"Okay, until we discover your musical talent, that's what we'll focus on. You'll shop for food, you'll use the cookbooks in the kitchen, and you'll make wonderful meals and lots of desserts. Fabulous desserts. That's how you'll spend your four hours here."

"Mr. Abram, can I ask a question?"

"Ask away."

"What will I be required to do with your toileting?"

"I toilet myself. Not that helpless, not yet. Don't worry. No diapers either."

4.

The apartment Ava lived in with her mother was on the first floor in the rear of the building. Most of the windows were on the air shaft so the light that came in was a wintry light thickened by dryer exhaust. When she first moved in, Cleopatra had commissioned a friend to make drapes. They were elaborately layered, as full as petticoats, gathered and drawn back with loopy bows. They so disguised the notion of an actual outside that it ceased even to be a concept, and in the once-elegant room, with the glass table and gold painted chairs at one end, the convertible sofa, BarcaLounger, TV, and coffee table at the other, the two overly dressed windows were like lidded eyes, pretending sleep, but spying on everything that took place.

Now that Ava had Mr. Abram's to go to, his clean, sun-lit rooms soothed the rage of the home apartment. She could walk past and not even see the open door of the hall closet that was too stuffed with Cleopatra's belongings to shut, the smoky air in the living room, or the clutter on tables that were never cleared.

Her mother returned from her job first, and by the time Ava got back, she had changed out of her bus-driver uniform into a slip and robe and settled herself in front of the TV for a night of movies. That was the routine. Her mother didn't care for news, game shows, or documentaries. She craved the neat, two-hour resolution of simple dramas and could watch two or three in an evening.

"What's that you got?"

Ava was toting groceries. "Dinner. I'm going to learn how to make vegetable soup."

"Just buy a can. It's always better. Plus it's more practical."

"I have to learn how to do it from scratch. With celery and carrots and tomatoes and stuff."

"Trust me, vegetables are a waste of money. You use a bit and the rest rots in the drawer."

"Well, not everyone agrees with that." She set the food on the counter, turned on the fluorescent and opened Mr. Abram's cookbook. Then she began washing and peeling.

"What, you're going to lug a pot of soup to his house?"

"No, this is practice. It's for you and me."

"No, baby. Homemade soup's gonna give me the runs. I need preservatives. They firm me up, keep me young."

"Mom, that's ridiculous."

"My ass! Who's the one hasn't had a cold in twenty years? Huh? Who's never taken a sick day? Huh, miss snivel-nose? How's the old man's hiney?"

"I wouldn't know. He takes care of toileting himself."

"Come in here so's you don't have to shout."

Ava stayed where she was, dribbled oil into a pan.

The lounger snapped forward and Cleopatra, holding a gold painted chair, appeared in the doorway. She set her wine glass on the shelf that held their pots and pans and sat down. "I bet it's all soft and saggy, just like what he's got in his front."

"I told you. He takes care of toileting himself."

"Listen to you, toileting. Where'd you get a word like that?"

"That's what they call it. Aides help with toileting, but he doesn't need it."

"Not yet," Cleopatra said, reaching for her glass. "But you wait. Everything changes. Like you. Gone all day, out somewheres I don't even know. With a new name. Grown up and everything and me back here by myself. Know what I want? Let's do Pictures."

"I can't, I've got to make this soup."

"After. When my movie's finished. Okay?"

The silence felt strange after the swell of romantic music signaling the movie's end. Ava carried their bowls to the table, set out bread and butter. Her mother sat down in a careful fashion, as though she were a guest at someone else's house. But the formality of having a proper meal, of facing each other across a table disappeared soon enough.

"There's not enough salt in here. And it needs way more pepper. But it's tasty. I think it's tasty."

"Is it okay? Is it thick enough?"

"I'm not the person to ask. Seems like canned is thicker. But thin soup's not terrible, it's good. Old people can't discriminate anyway."

"I want it to be really good. I think I should have added more spice."

"Spice is complicated. Watch out. Pass the saltines?" Cleopatra crumbled a stack of crackers into her bowl. "Now that's the ticket, that makes it like gumbo."

When they were done, Ava filled the sink with detergent. Cleo called, "Come back, baby. Dishes can wait; sit on the couch, here, next to your mama."

So Ava came in and collapsed against the pillowed mass of the familiar body. It was always a relief to give in. She could revert, deny all she'd been attempting, as though the process of becoming a different person were simply a game for the outside world. At their first apartment they had shared a double bed, but when she was eleven, they moved to this apartment because there was a separate bedroom for Ava. That's when Pictures had started. It was a carry-over of the old closeness, a way to snuggle together and be one body again though with Pictures the body they considered was a fiction. They sat side by side with the album on their laps and looked at Cleo as she used to be.

"There I was in the bumble bee costume. Look at my shape, will you?"

The script was always the same: "You must have weighed, what? A hundred pounds?"

"Hundred and fifteen," Cleo said proudly, "but look, I had boobs. That's why I was so spectacular. A little thing but knockers the size of grapefruit."

Their only photo album chronicled a single year in the life of Cleopatra Prett before Ava, née Marilyn, was even a blink in the universe. "Look at that! Will you look at that? What a keister! You see, I had these swivel hips and if they were playing something slow, something bluesy? You should have seen me. I could hypnotize them with my slow, sexy hips. Look at that ass. I loved this striped one. Leaves nothing to the imagination. Of all those dancers, and there we are lined up, I got the most applause. They knew quality. Those old drunks, they knew quality."

They were black and whites, all from 1959, the year she had worked at a club in midtown. She would have worked there longer, but violations had shut it down. Drug trafficking, prostitution? Or was it something neutral like not enough fire exits? Cleopatra had never said. Violations was as specific as she got. When they arrived at the last photograph, which was of a beaming young woman doing a split in the center of a tiny stage, she would expel a sound of regret and touch the photo. "I was making good money, all under the table. Not like now when half goes to the government. Plus tips. Oh, did I make tips! But the very next day, the day after that photo, the Feds busted the joint and my career was over. I went to Miami and tried to get started there, but Florida, it was hard if you weren't Cuban. And now, look at me. Dressed like a man every day of my waking life."

"But you *like* driving," Ava reminded her.

"I do. I like sitting up in that seat and having all the power. But that was a glamour life. Your old mother, she had a glamour life."

What Ava wanted to ask was off the script. "Could you tell me? Please, Mom, now that I'm graduated and have a job?"

Cleo sighed, lit a cigarette. "I know you want to know. It hurts not knowing, I know it does, and I wish I could tell you. There's nothing I wish for more."

"You know who your boyfriend was. So that's my dad, isn't it?"

"Look. I wish it was different. I wish I had the answer. I wish I could just say a name. But there's lots of women, this problem is not unique. How you going to know which person's genes the one that made your child? They just pretend. I don't pretend. I've always lived by the truth and I ain't about to stop doing it now. They were multiples, you understand? Multiples. Now that you're graduated, that's what I can tell you. It wasn't just one at a time. So ease off." She set her cigarette in the closest of the living room's many ashtrays and stood up, easing her swollen feet into her slippers. "Because it's starting to feel like criticism. The changing name thing, the who is my father thing, the gone all day at work thing, so when I come home there's no one here and the place feels like death. It does. It does. It feels like death until you get back."

These were the moments she loved her. The mixture of guilt, remorse, and fear was a syrup that loosened her resolve, tempting her to deny everything that she was trying to become, making it easy to slide back to being her mother's child, only her mother's child. But she steeled herself to resist it. Wrapping her arms around the warmth and plush she said, "I'm sorry, Mom, but I have to grow up."

And yet, the body young Cleo had flaunted in booze-soaked clubs scared the daughter. It also embarrassed her and made her shy.

Though very occasionally, when she was alone, the fear would slide away. She'd lift her chest, let her hips drop down, and with her breath, she'd pull up from the hard ground she was walking on, a feeling of rhythm. She couldn't let it break out if it was summertime, but if it were winter and a jacket covered her hips, she gave herself permission. Then her joints would loosen and the ordinary act of being a pedestrian turned so audacious she would worry that a man might give her trouble. In jacket weather, when she was captured by the rhythm, she would walk instead of taking the subway just to feel it. The undulation, the outrageous switch and sway.

5.

It was back! The flicker of possibility! Back again after so many years. But now it stayed north, making him as light and giddy as a divine being. In the old days, when everything shot south, he had to fight the distraction of lust. Because possibility was fickle. That sudden vision of what a person was capable of, that fragile, shimmering belief, that tiny ping had to be treated with the greatest respect, nurtured and fed till it could stand on its own and be heard. So even in the old days desire stayed separate. He was as superstitious as an old witch doctor. The shimmering had to be strong, the talent fact before he could relax. Then he was good.

Of course, the possibilities of Ava Prett were a perfect zero. Couldn't sing, couldn't cook, couldn't hold much of a conversation, knew nothing about music. And yet there was eagerness. Where did that come from?

Every day now, knowing she would arrive, he woke up more easily. Of course, by the time she left, he was ready to be by himself again, but the next morning, there he was, anxious for her to appear again.

Jennifer was concerned about her inexperience. Wondered if they should ask the agency to send someone older, someone who knew how to cook so he lied and said, "She's a great cook. Pot pies, meatballs, roasts. I'm eating like a gourmet. Pretty soon I won't be able to fit into my clothes."

"Tell her please, use real butter. You need the fat, you're too thin."

"I guarantee she went through a pound of butter last week. Shortbread cookies: that's her specialty."

"And she's how old?"

The skepticism was clear so he answered, "Eighteen," and then embroidered a tale. "She went to one of those high schools that train for careers, you know, they're very popular here, and she was in culinary arts."

"Really? That's lucky. See, what did I tell you? And she's honest? You like her?"

She would call Maxi Bruder to get confirmation. And that wily old bitch would read Ava Prett like a page of print. She'd see her lack of skill right away, sniff out her inexperience. And Bruder would have no trouble recognizing deceit. He could ask her to lie to Jennifer, but nothing would be more appealing to a dishonest woman than the chance to be a double agent. So the only solution was in Ava herself.

They began each day with tea in the living room. He was waiting at the table, watching her through the doorway, pretending to read the Times, but really he was adrift in the sounds of another person. They were so beautiful he wondered if now, those sounds were the only sounds he needed, if ordinary busyness were the only music old age required. But a young person's busyness. Maxi's once-a-week bustling was not a pleasure at all. A young person, unformed.

When she came in with the tray, he thought there was no more pleasing shape than a teapot. A teapot with two cups beside it, heaven. (You doddy old man, you're absolutely pathetic.)

"It's going to clear up later and get nice," she told him, setting a plate of toast on the mat in front of him, each slice buttered, and a little dollop of marmalade in a pretty cup. "Do you ever go outside?"

"Only for doctor's appointments."

"Don't you miss it?"

"I did, earlier, but now I don't think about it at all. With my windows, I get the sky."

"But you need more than that. Don't you? Wouldn't you like to see trees? How hard would it be?"

"You'd have to push me."

"I'm pretty strong. We could go to the park."

"It's a bit of a slog coming back. You're not *that* strong." He saw her disappointment and relented. "Okay, we'll try it. But today there's a more pressing matter." He looked at her, assessing his chances. "I have to prepare you for a little performance. What do you think of that?" Her forehead was clear. No lines of worry, no consternation. Was it simply her age, or was she more naïve than most?

"It starts tomorrow and every Thursday afternoon after that. That's when Mrs. Bruder shows up. Housekeeper and spy. My daughter is concerned that being so young you might be a little inexperienced. She wants to get someone in here who can cook."

"Oh! I've learned vegetable soup! I'm going to make it for you today. I practiced last night and it was good. Or at least I thought it was!"

"Well, I'm afraid it has to be more than that. Pot pies, shortbread cookies, roast chicken, waldorf salad. Rich, buttery, Jewish meals. I told her you'd been to culinary school. Also, we have to work on attitude. Make you less timid. Turn you into someone that Mrs. Bruder, a formidable busybody who reports directly to Jennifer, will not want to cross. Attitude, you see, comes from confidence which you, my dear, possess very little of. Which is appropriate for your age," he added quickly, seeing her despair. "So what we're going to do is add just a little bit of arrogance into your personality. Okay? Not much. We won't overdo it."

He couldn't tell what she was thinking and marveling at her ability to seem so agreeable, he went on. "Mrs. Bruder is very prompt, comes at one, leaves at four. And for those three hours we're going to make you a different person. You'll mostly be in the kitchen, but she'll have to come in to mop the floor. It will be enormously annoying for you, but you'll put up with it. You will signal that to her. All right? We'll plan on roast chicken with rosemary and onions and a rich gravy."

"But I've never roasted a chicken in my life."

"Everyone can roast a chicken. Even if, despite decades of sublimation and diaspora your genes were never polluted, which was how they would have thought of it, with the genes of a Jew." (You show-off! What's the result of all of this fancy talk? Huh? Nothing will ensure her quiet faster than that.)

And it did. She was meek and submissive and he schooled her all day long: what to wear, how to talk.

"You're the boss here. Okay? So show me how you're the boss." Playing the part of Maxi he said, "Mr. Abram, how am I supposed to clean when she's in there cooking? This won't work. It's me or her. We both can't be here."

Ava didn't even try. "I don't know what to say."

"Say something. What about anger?"

She put her hands on her hips in an unconvincing way and in an unnatural tone proclaimed as though she were reading a script: "I'm sorry. Mr. Abram hired me to cook for him and that's what I have to do."

"No!" he cried. "She'll know it's an act. You're not *in* it. Remember: you're a great cook and you have no patience. Okay. Try again."

"I'm sorry, Mrs. Bruder, but we'll have to work it out."

"No patience, remember?" But it was hopeless. She had no talent, not a glimmer, not a seed of the ability to transform. He wheeled himself into the music room and put on Mary Lou Williams playing piano in a Chicago club where none of the fat cats thought a woman was worth listening to. It was 1930 and her heart was in her fingers. It had to be if she were going to get through that door. He turned the sound up. "This woman has a body!" he called to Ava. "She's in her body and she's talking about what that feels like. That's what you have to do. Feel the rhythm. It's your heartbeat. Your heart swings. See?" He didn't even know if she could hear him. "They stole my legs you see, so now all I've got is my chest, my shoulders, my arms, my head. But I'm feeling it." He was positioned where he could look out of the windows and and move just for himself and the birds and the bats, just him and the holy audience of the trees along Central Park West. He moved for the trees. And when the song was over (and why did it have to end?) he lifted the needle, and there was a deep and pure cessation of everything he had been feeling and in a calm and infinitely patient voice he said, "Try it again." He didn't shout it, but he turned around and saw that she was standing behind him. He said Maxi's lines, she said hers, and she was just as stiff and wooden as before.

So maybe it wouldn't work. Maybe it would all go to bust and he would be back to where he was, which was alone, and after all, that was his preference. And she would be elsewhere. Where, he wondered, but he couldn't, for even a moment, imagine another place that someone as ineffective as her might go to.

"Don't I have to cook something?" she asked.

"Indeed you do," he said with as much enthusiasm as he could muster. But it was all a bust. He went through the motions. He sent her down to the street with a list of ingredients for the market where he had a credit and with his credit card to a clothing store. He could imagine Jennifer on that subject. *You sent her out with your credit card?*

She came back with so many bags she could hardly get through the door. Did you find something?" he asked, and after she stashed a big bag in the closet, carried the other ones to the kitchen, (putting his credit card and the receipts on the counter first thing), she said, "I think so." He didn't ask for more information. She wasn't his daughter, after all. So he watched as she unwrapped a chicken. She rinsed and dried it and set it on a plate. He talked her through how to prepare it for roasting, how to make gravy without lumps, how to mash potatoes. He forbid her to write anything down. "Just listen," he said. "Picture each step as I describe it. Picture yourself doing it. Be in your body. Dream about it tonight and by tomorrow, we'll see."

She looked uncertain.

"You will roast that chicken so it will be the best roast chicken it can possibly be. You are the one who knows how to do that. Be arrogant." There. He was done. He looked at her for confirmation and her expression was eager but vacant. The lack of attitude unsettled him.

But by one o'clock the next day, the apartment was filled with a delicious odor. Maxi eased her bulk plus all of her satchels and packages through the door. "Someone's cooking?" So he wheeled out and Ava came forward, wiping floury hands on her apron. "It's so lovely to meet you!" she cried, flashing that big, ridiculously wholesome smile, thrusting her small white hand towards a startled Mrs. Bruder.

"Whatch you cookin here? Smells mighty good." She walked towards the kitchen, but Ava ran to intercept. "Sorry! Off-limits! Got a million things going on and everything's measured out. Cookie batter, gravy, salad dressing. All happening."

"Well how am I supposed to clean?"

"I'm sorry, but there can't be any interruptions. Everything's timed to the minute. Maybe. . . ." She stared off into space. "How long are you here?"

"I have to leave by four or I miss my bus."

"Well, that would work. I'll get out of your way at three forty five. You can have fifteen minutes. That should be plenty of time, sweep the floor, mop. I'll do counters and dishes as I go. Will that work for you?" Hand on her hips, she made it clear there was only one answer.

"If you keep your end, I keep mine."

"All right then." She patted her tightly blue jeaned butt and turned around, leaving the housekeeper startled and him in a blur of surprise and love.

6.

He hadn't said what she should spend. Or even what he wanted her to get. *Can you find yourself some clothes that will make you look older? Slimmer pants, maybe? Something more...* he had paused to choose the word *...robust for a blouse? Walk along Broadway, you'll find something.* The pants were easy. She found a pair of jeans that were tighter than what she normally wore. But the top she was unsure about. Robust? How could a blouse be robust?

Cleopatra had trained her to buy only from the sales racks. Still, there was a lot to look through. She didn't like spangly or sparkly, she didn't like tight or low-cut. She looked at one ugly thing after another, getting more and more agitated. She was wasting his time. So maybe pants would be good enough and she should just give up on the blouse. Gathering her purse, the pants she was going to buy, she headed towards the cashier and it was while she was standing in line that she flashed on Cleopatra's photo album. There was her model. That was the woman she was supposed to become.

So she went back to the sales racks and as she pushed the hangers aside, she saw the blouse she should have. It was made of a stretchy, sparkly material with puffy sleeves and a deep neckline. It made her look chesty and maybe that was what he meant by robust. She bought five plastic bangles for her wrist and the next day, in alien clothes and bangled arms she became Cleopatra of the kitchen. It was easy; she became the very person she had been trying all of her life to escape.

Over the next month he sent her out twice to buy clothes. She didn't see the necessity, but he said Maxi would get suspicious if she wore the same thing every week. She couldn't take her new clothes home (how would she explain?) so she kept them in a plastic bag at the top of Harvey's closet and wore them only on Thursdays.

One day, late in the afternoon, the door opened and a big man swept in and started to sing. "Isn't it bliss? Don't you approve? One who keeps tearing around, one who can't move." He had a beautiful voice, but that was all he sang. Then he twirled and laughed and leaned down to untie his shoes.

Ava came out of the kitchen.

"Ava Gardner, pleased to meet you. I'm Peter Finch." He noticed her shocked expression and said quickly, "No, no, not at all. I am, at the moment, an underemployed choreographer named Ruben. But I have some prospects and I've come to see my dad. Where is the old man?" He held out his hand, gave hers a polite shake, and then skated in socks down Bruder's hallway. Ava heard them go into the music room and as she worked in the kitchen, she heard laughter and music drift out. Salmon was grilling in the broiler and she was chopping vegetables for a noodle salad, something she was inventing on the spot. *Experiment! I've given you a good foundation. All you have to do now is get creative. Butter, thyme, rosemary for meat, okay? Olive oil and dill for vegetables and fish. Pepper for everything, white and black, and paprika always. Salt for some things. Taste and use your judgment.*

She heard the music change. Now it was faster, more energetic, happy. "No, that's not right either," Ruben cried.

There was more discussion. The wheelchair creaked over the floorboards and then something slow came out of the speakers. A sad, lonely voice. But it wasn't a voice; it was an instrument.

"Maybe."

"Slow is always better."

"I don't know, Dad. Maybe it is when you're eighty five."

"Ha! You're wrong about that. Slow is always better."

"But I wasn't thinking blues."

The dishes were done; the counters were clean, the salad finished, and all she was waiting for was the fish. *Till it flakes,* he told her.

"The man and the woman could move in opposite directions away from each other. Why not take over the entire space? Something like…."

She heard some shuffles and Harvey said, "Yeah, like that."

It flaked. So she turned off the oven and put some shortbread on a plate to carry in to them.

Ruben was twirling around on one foot, a shock of bleached hair, arms roped with muscles, hands open in the air. She stood at the doorway and when he saw her, Ruben paused.

"Oh! Sorry! I just thought that maybe you would want some

cookies. I'm really sorry to interrupt. I was just wondering … well, cookies! Anyway, sorry again. I'll see you tomorrow."

"Nice to meet you!" Ruben cried, turning back to his father, dismissing her. But Harvey said, "Wait a minute. All we need's a body. She can't dance, but at least you can see how it will work."

"Dad, I'm sure she has somewhere to get to."

Harvey said, "Ava, can you give us half an hour or so?"

"Oh! I was just going to slip out."

"Fifteen minutes? Ruben, tell her what you want."

"Dad, really, this is an imposition."

"It's all right. Tell her."

Facing her, Ruben said, "So… you have the time?"

"Sure," she said, feeling herself blush.

"Ever do any dancing?"

But Harvey answered. "Dancing won't work with her. Just a body."

"Okay, so something really simple, a triple step, triple step. We're going to glide two steps, triple step, triple step, glide two steps, triple step, triple step. Like that. Just do the best you can, nothing matters. So, Dad, music again, we'll hold hands facing each other, triple step, triple step, and then when I tell you, we'll start to move apart, triple step, triple step. Ready?" He held out his hands and she took hold, facing him.

As soon as the music started he began to bounce softly in place. "See? Like this. Feel it."

She bounced the way he did and it felt good, she could do it. They began to move apart, farther, farther. She kept herself in check. All in control.

"Good, you've got the step, good." And then after they crossed the floor back again Harvey said, "Ava, try putting attitude in it."

"Dad, don't push. It doesn't matter. It's only practice and she's fine as. . . ."

But Harvey didn't wait for him to finish. "Ava," he said, "do Thursday."

That was all she needed. Her hips got loose, her steps got small and sticky, and her chest filled with her mother's hatred for these two men.

"Now we triple step back towards each other, triple step, triple step, till we're facing and I do a dip. Okay?" She faced him and without any pause he moved into her body and held it more gently than anyone had ever held her. "Trust me," he whispered. She wanted to crush him. She let all of her weight go into his arms, but it didn't hurt him at all; he lowered her down, all the way to the floor, and then back up.

Harvey clapped. "How'd it feel?" he asked, looking at Ruben.

"Actually, it felt good. I think it's the right tempo. Thank you, Ava," he said, and turning back to his dad he asked, "How did it look?"

"Great. Go with the slow. It has more sex in it. I'll see you tomorrow," Harvey called as Ava backed out. She finished up and peeked into the room before leaving. They were deep in conversation, one grey head next to one blonde and the cookies were untouched. Very quietly, she let herself out the door.

7.

The chicken was too dry, too salty. It had a beautifully crisp skin, but she'd cooked it too long and the breast meat was tasteless. The salmon was done to perfection. The next day he showed her how to make mayonnaise and then taught her to mix it with yogurt and garlic and dill to get a light, zesty, sauce, perfect for cold fish.

He had parked himself, and he did use that word, because with the chair he was more of a vehicle than a man, and angles, turns, spacing were things he had to consider. So he had parked himself at the widest part of the galley kitchen and she did what he told her mostly with her back to him, moving from refrigerator to stove, to sink, to cutting board. She was getting better with the knife. Could almost dice like a professional.

But it was too intimate. Her awkward elbows, the movement of her shoulder blades, the downward tilt of her head so the long white neck was revealed to him, brushed by that thick, blunt hair. He didn't oogle. That part was retired. Without regrets. They'd had a good time, he and his libido and now, without it, he felt smarter, more attentive. But he watched.

"How do you know about this?" she asked.

He laughed.

"You're like an expert."

"I was a good cook, I will say that. But it's easy. Once you know a few basic things: mayonnaise, béchamel sauce, roasting, stewing, how to use spices, it's wide open. Pie crust."

"Your wife didn't cook?"

"No, she had no feel for it. I think she would have been content living on take-out. People do that, you know."

She never took the bait. Someone else might have said, Oh we get take-out all the time. But with her, absolutely nothing of her other life escaped. Oddly, it turned him into a teacher: *This is how people talk to one another. This is how they become friends. They reveal things about themselves. Like this:*

"My wife. You know her name, Alice. Alice Long. She did three things in her life besides being wife and mother. She sang, she travelled for her career, and she attended to her looks. I managed her career. That's how we met. I discovered her and was her agent. She managed her beauty."

"How can a person manage beauty?" she asked. "Aren't they just beautiful or not beautiful?"

"Well, that's what you might think. But beauty can be enhanced. Everyone has it, some people simply need to coax it out. Alice was a nice looking woman to start with. She had good hair, good facial structure, but she always felt she was too heavy in the buttocks, and of course, she wanted more bosom. Women are never satisfied. You must know that, don't you?"

She ran the chopping knife under the spigot and moved from chopping onion to garlic. "I don't know. I feel like I don't really know how I look. I mean, what the mirror shows you depends on the lighting. I look terrible under fluorescents."

"For Alice, how she looked was a constant occupation. Facials, manicures, clothes, makeup. The whole bit. She did exercises every morning, walked a mile a day at least. She never took taxis. Not even if it was raining.

"Alice wanted to hire a cook. Ruben was small, and we were very busy. But I had a better idea. I bought a couple of cookbooks and I taught myself and once I learned a few things we ate well, we really did, and it wasn't that much effort. I cooked in quantity so it would last a few days."

When she moved to the sink he saw neat piles of chopped vegetables. "The mayonnaise?" she prompted.

"Ah, the mystery! Unless you're a physicist, of course. But how is it that by blending three loose ingredients, egg, oil, lemon juice, you create a substance that is solid? Common people, like us, who don't know the laws of behavior, can be awed by simple transformation. So go ahead, start the machine, now pour one half cup oil in very slowly, a thin stream. Then the lemon juice. You'll start to see it coagulate."

"It's coagulating." She tilted the bowl of the Cuisinart and mayonnaise swirled into a container, coaxed by her rubber spatula.

"So you met Ruben," he began.

"He's nice. He and your daughter, they're the only kids?"

"Ruben's adopted and Jennifer was a surprise."

"Oh."

He watched her put it all together. Some people, like her, processed things on their own. You could never be sure what they truly thought because it was so recessed. But he saw, or he thought he saw, a click of interest. Something about *her* parentage? They had decided it would not be a secret. So they spoke frankly about Ruben's birth family, that his mother wasn't stable, that his father had disappeared, and when Ruben turned thirteen, he decided to see his mother again. Even now he still visited her, maybe once or twice a year.

"Okay, so now the other things?"

"Taste it yourself and decide."

"Well, garlic and dill definitely. I'm not sure if onion would be good."

"Trust your instincts. Use the onion for something else. We didn't get him as a baby. He was eight years old, in foster care. Not thriving. Had been moved around a lot among relatives, none of whom you would call sober, settled people, then from one foster home to another. When we got him, he was…." (a little shit, but he didn't say that.) "Combative. Fists up at everything. That whole first year we were sure we'd made a terrible mistake. Or I had made it, because from the beginning Alice wanted a baby. I thought we were too old to start with babies. Ha! Little did I know. Jennifer showed up two years later. That's why I started cooking. Kept me at home more, with him. We did it together. We learned it together."

"So he's a good cook too?"

"Terrible. Never learned anything. Hates it even now."

"Okay, so everything's ready."

In the living room they helped themselves to the elegant lunch she had prepared. Life! The sounds of silverware on dishes, the clink of the serving platter set back onto the table. He wished she weren't so quiet. What was his incessant conversation but a tactic to get her to talk? He spooned sauce over the cold fish and took the first bite. A beautiful pairing of texture and taste. The greeny zest of dill, the bite of garlic. He made a silent plea: Please don't let me die in a hospital, far from the experience of well-prepared food.

"I have congestive heart failure. Did you know that? I couldn't remember if I'd told you. Medicines help stabilize me, but I could go any time. So I'm warning you. You could be out of a job. But at least you'll know something about cooking. It wouldn't all have been a waste."

"Oh, it's not a waste at all," she said simply. "Don't die yet. I like you." But after she made that statement, she turned red as a beet.

He chuckled. "Well, I'll do my best." He could see she wanted to change the subject, but he wasn't going to help her. The afterglow was too lovely and *I like you* had to be the most beautiful sentence in the language. Better than love, really, because it was cleaner, more simple. There was no ownership, no greed.

"So what does Ruben do?"

He coughed, holding the napkin to his mouth because like most old men, coughing released spittle, and now that she liked him, he mustn't be disgusting.

"I'm so sorry! We should have explained last night."

"He told me. But I didn't know what it meant."

"Choreographer? He gets hired to design dances for musical theater. And he's not a bad actor or singer either. But he's a great dancer and that's his first love."

"I didn't know a person could be a dancer. I mean, a legitimate dancer." She was beet red again. "I mean, not a stripper or a showgirl."

"Oh yes, Ruben's first year here when he was angry and mouthy and just an all-around little fuck, excuse my language" (she smiled at that) "we told him he couldn't waste our time. He had to work at something. He had to become something. He had to discover what he was good at."

"That seems like a lot of pressure."

"It was. But this kid needed a kick in the butt. He had to learn that being resentful would get him nowhere. So we said, choose one thing to do. Actually, it was even more pressure than that. Choose one thing to be good at, is what we said. And we gave him a list of the usual things: art, music, science, woodworking, sports, and he chose sports. 'Basketball,' he said. That made sense, even then he was a tall, lanky kid. But it didn't work. I'm not sure why. So Alice said, and this was her brilliance, 'what was it that attracted you to basketball?'

'Jumping,' he told her." (His pugilistic way of standing in the room, the make-me glare of those hard, adolescent eyes.)

"Alice got a flash. 'He means dance,' she said to me. So she said, 'how about jumping to music?' And he said he would like that. So we signed him up for tap classes. That was Alice's brilliance again. 'This kid needs to make noise. He's never still. He wants you to know he's there.' And she was absolutely right. Because from the beginning, he was very good at it."

And then something slipped out of the locked box. Ava laid her fork down and said, "I wish I had parents like you. I'm not good at anything."

Well, he wasn't much of a romantic. When the woman you love dies at age sixty three, you lose a certain amount of trust in the goodness of the world. It was Alice who could save people. He was not good at it. But he felt Ava's eyes on him and he knew that the tiny bit of information she'd let out was huge. So he told a lie. And he convinced himself, before saying it, that this was not saving someone, particularly since it could backfire completely. But he took a chance. He said, "You could be a dancer too. Ruben said you were so relaxed in his arms and you picked up the rhythm so effortlessly, he thought you had real talent."

"Really? He said that? Wow, I've never thought about it."

'Well, what *have* you thought about?" That was too peremptory. So he asked more softly, "What have you imagined yourself doing?"

"You're going to laugh, especially after what you told me. But I was really good at it in school and I love watching it on TV."

He waited.

She cleared her throat and then she said, "Basketball."

"Well, women's basketball is a very big sport."

"It is, but I don't think it's for me."

"One thing I told Alice when she was starting out. Don't waste your time with doubt."

"But Alice had talent. Some people don't have talent."

He watched her load the dishes onto a black mother of pearl tray they had bought many years ago in Portugal. Alice had found it in a cluttered shop near their hotel. "Everyone has talent. There is something they are good at."

She laughed in the kitchen. Then he heard the spring of the dishwasher door opening. And for a moment he felt sorry for himself.

Such a cruel about-face. To have nobody of promise on the horizon, and why would he, he hadn't been active in eight years, and now who was he spending his days with? A human person who believed she was worthless.

8.

Harvey was at the cardiologist's and Ava was going to surprise him with a dinner she'd cooked entirely on her own. She'd been studying one of his cookbooks and the market on Broadway where Harvey kept an account had fresh crab.

"The year I lived in Miami," Cleopatra liked to tell her, "I ate nothing but crab cakes. They were so cheap. You could buy them anywhere and crab isn't fattening. A couple of crab cakes, a couple of beers, I was set for the night. It was good too because they didn't make me gassy. Those little outfits, let me tell you, they hugged the tummy and if you had any bit of bloat, and I got bloat as easily then as I do now, you're sunk."

She chopped the crab, the scallion, the parsley. She made the sauce that went with it, something French she couldn't pronounce. And then she heard a quick knock on the door and saw it opening.

"Ava, it's Ruben."

The knife slipped out of her wet fingers. "In the kitchen," she called, bending down.

"Hey, do you know what time Dad gets back?" He slid across the foyer and came to a dramatic, tottering stop, a forelock of blond hair over his face.

"Around four. But he said it's unpredictable with that doctor."

"Good! Well, so what are you making?"

"Crab cakes. Do you know if he likes them?"

"Just happens to be his all-time favorite. What he always used to get when we went to the seashore."

The counters were clean, the floor was swept, and if she had been alone, she probably would have sat down with a magazine. The only thing left to do was sauté the patties, and she'd do that at the last minute so they'd still be warm for dinner. So she asked Ruben if he'd like tea and cookies.

"No thank you, Ava." Quickly, not even looking at her, shuffling through the albums in the music room. So she stood there for a little bit, uncomfortably. "You can watch, darling," he said, and gestured her into a chair.

Darling! No one had ever called her that. She sat down, prepared for him to ignore her.

"I'm trying to work out some ideas. Dad has the best music library in the whole city, so I'm just sampling things."

There was a single horn, a trumpet she thought. It cried out to her. He moved in slow, fluid motions, which was exactly what the horn wanted him to do because it was slow and fluid too. He was counting out loud, stopping and starting, repeating the first phrases of the song over and over. He was so absorbed she couldn't look away. And then he sank onto the floor, legs out, back against the wall. But he jumped up and went to the kitchen for a glass of water. He was slicked with sweat and he drank quickly.

"Dad says he's been teaching you how to cook. He says you're learning really fast. You know, we were so afraid you'd be another Mrs. Bruder. But you're great for him. I think he was kind of depressed before and another Bruder would have sent him to the loony bin."

"He's been so entirely nice."

"Well, Dad sings your praises too. So what do you want to do, besides this, I mean?"

"Oh! You mean like a career? Just this. I really like it."

Ruben took his glasses off and massaged the bridge of his nose with his fingers. "Wow, it's been a long day." He put his head down for a moment and the blond forelock fell over his face. He seemed to be thinking. "Want to try something? This little combo I'm working out? I think it's cute. Especially for a gamine like you. Here, let me demonstrate."

"I can't," she said. "I have to cook."

"Just for a minute," he said, guiding her into a series of steps. It was terrifying. She could feel the empty apartment around them, the pressure of all of the money and talent that had created it and kept it going, things that were alien to her, and beauty, Alice's beauty. She got the steps. She got the rhythm, but movement was impossible. He stopped the music and said, "When you were like this last time, a little robotic, not very relaxed, Dad said 'do Thursday' and you got all loose and curvy. Can you do Thursday again?"

"I don't know. I feel nervous."

"Just listen. Just move with me. Don't think."

She summoned Cleopatra from the photo album. She imagined the smoky bar, the lonely men watching her, and she began to move her hips in time to the beat. It was strange. She felt as though she knew exactly where the music was going to go. She could hear a pattern and somehow she knew how to translate it to movement. There was a drum roll and without any planning, her pelvis swung slowly in and out, making a figure eight. She had ceased to exist. There was only the armature of his body moving with hers. Ruben supported her weight in his arms and as she relaxed into them, he lowered her to the floor in a dip. She dropped her head, though it wasn't her head any longer, it was someone else's, and she drew a slow, sexy leg towards her body as smoothly as though this were a move she'd been doing all her life.

The song ended. Ruben hooted. And when she looked up, Harvey was parked at the door, applauding.

"I want to use her," Ruben said to his father. "I like her better than Violet. What would you say, Ava? A possibility? Three weeks of evening rehearsals? It's off-Broadway and it could close quickly, or it could catch hold and have a long run."

9.

The studio was in an old factory. There was a large room with a scrubbed wooden floor, tall windows, and the ancient scent of machine oil from the days when there were monolithic iron beasts stamping or printing or doing some other mechanized, repetitive task. There were tracks on the ceiling, pulleys and chains on the back wall, and a half dismantled iron structure. A setting for a horror film. Night filled the windows, the autumn air leaking through, and light bulbs hung from rafters. She was terrified. The five other people scattered about the room were older and she could tell they were experienced. They would hate her, she was so inept.

The chairs along the wall were draped with jackets; bags and shoes were scattered about. She chose an empty seat and while she was unlacing her boots, her fingers shaking with nervousness, a woman galloped across the floor towards her, a wide, child-like grin on her face. "Ruben's treasure! Welcome! I'm Brekka!" And then she said, "Oh dear, I'm sorry." She gathered her long hair, wrapped it around her hand and secured it with a rubber. "Let me start again. You're Ava, the aide for Ruben's father. Welcome to the dance factory. As Ruben likes to say, we still manufacture, but now it's the business of dreams." Brekka held out both her hands and as Ava placed her trembling fingers in the older woman's firm grasp, she said, surprising herself, "I'm so scared!"

"I'll tell you a secret. We're all terrified because this is a new piece. But I'm here if you need me, and Ruben's very patient, very kind. Shall I show you some warm-ups? We don't have many rules around here but you must never start cold. Always stretch first. And here, I brought some extra leggings because it will be awhile before the room heats up."

Ava followed Brekka out to the floor and took a spot behind her to copy the stretches. Soon the door banged open and Ruben swept in, slipping out of his coat, throwing down his bag. He took off his street shoes and walked to the center, his large, strong strides bouncing the floor. The dancers moved in to greet him.

"Hello you wonderful people! Thank you for being so prompt. There is a new woman here and some of you returning people haven't been together in awhile, so we'll begin with introductions." He said a few sentences about each person and for Ava he said, "This is her first exposure to musical theater so help her out when you can." Then he stood quietly for a moment, hands clasped in a prayer position, and began to talk. "Okay, so the dances are going to mime urban life. They are meant to be stylized and that's why we're going to exaggerate and ham it up and use props. High heels, hats, briefcases, pocketbooks. And for the hippies: beads, dangles, feathers and stuff like that. We won't get into costumes until later, but we'll start with props from the beginning and you'll see how necessary they are. The tempo will shift from slow and bluesy to fast and staccato. It's set in Times Square and the theme is contrasts. I have copies of the script here. Ava is with us because I needed someone who looked really young for one of the roles. And she is young. Didn't you just graduate high school?"

"In June," she said, and to her horror, they clapped.

"So, I want to give you the general shape of the story because what's going to be immensely important to us is attitude. As you know, each dancer has two roles, and attitude is going to be what differentiates them. It's as important as costume changes. More important, actually."

Ava wondered how you could do attitude if you didn't have lines. Or a specific person to convince. Playing two roles would make it even harder. But Ruben was watching her, so she attempted to settle her face, attempted to look confident. That was when she realized she played two roles at Harvey's; she even did it well.

"The banker will also be the pimp, the runaway will be the prostitute, the mother will be the alcoholic. The message is that people are not so different and what goes on in the darkness in the dirty movie theater is the same as what goes on in the executive office of the bank. Here's how it starts: A band of street performers set up in Times Square. They live in a brightly painted van, hide from the police, and survive on donations. That's who we are. They make music, dance, chant, but they're not saints by any means. They have a child in their midst, a runaway who sleeps with the guys in the band. A banker who walks through the square everyday to get to his office, lusts for the runaway and drags her into his car. She's traumatized, winds up becoming a street-walker. That's the basic set-up."

"How's it end?" someone called.

Ruben laughed. "Well, I know you're impatient, but like Broadway, it's gotta please everyone, so there's tragedy and happiness. The pimp gets caught with drugs and goes to jail. That frees the runaway. Then the producer sees the performers, likes what he sees, and gives them a legitimate theater run and for a little while, they're stars." Ruben twirled around, did a little two step. "The music is really exciting. We sing but not lyrics. We make sounds with our voices, and with junk that's lying around. We beat plastic buckets, car parts, lamp posts, and we stomp and tap with our shoes. We're always keeping a percussion, a rhythm. Sammo is the only one who has songs with lyrics. But the movements will be challenging and I promise you we're going to work our tails off."

"Ruben, can I say something? About the script?" Justin Beckwith, the dancer who would play Sammo, stepped forward. "Not to throw cold water on anything or question your judgment, but it seems a little too tame. I mean, I read it and there's not much there if you ask me."

Ava was shocked, but Ruben chuckled. He even gave Justin a little salute. "Right! It's thin, thin, thin and I'm glad you brought that up. Here's my take: Musical theater works best when the plot is simple, when the narrative has a predictable arc. The audience can't be figuring stuff out; they have to get it all quickly so they can give their attention to the textures of what's happening, that is, the sounds and movements, the great delicious *how* of the story. The real beauty of this production is that the music and dance happen within the context of street performance. We're not also speaking lines. We're only the chorus. Only! Nothing only about it. It's the chorus that will carry the show."

That first night, Ruben taught the men their major combos and Brekka taught the women. She began with the secretary dance, a staccato rhythm, high heels tapping loudly, the steps tiny and repetitive. "You'll be moving up and down a series of stairs. We'll get those in here next week. Underneath the stair forms, Ava, as the runaway first, and then as prostitute, will be slinking around. Secretaries, keep going! Now Ava...." Brekka turned to her, her small breasts perfectly outlined by her leotard, her big hands moving as she spoke. "You're lithe and limber and absolutely free with your body. You're like a flower blowing in the wind and you've got splits and somersaults. I'll teach you those moves, but for tonight, we're going to do your major sequence which is this..." She arched her back, thrust her chest out, and made triple step circles leading with the hip. It was a development of the combo she first did with Ruben. "Follow me," Brekka instructed. "You secretaries, don't stop. It's all simultaneous. No Ava, make it more, exaggerate those hips. Yes, that's better. Sexpot! That's how the runaway survives. Think sexpot. Your movements can't be like the secretaries. Your attitude is different."

At the end, Brekka gave her a hug and whispered, "You did great. I have no worries. Just make that your definition."

"You mean sexpot. . . .?"

"Yes, that's your mantra."

A few of the others came up and said, "good job," as Ava was putting on her street shoes, and after everyone else left, Ruben sidled over and sat down next to her, slipping his big feet out of dance shoes and lacing up boots. "Is this going to work for you?"

"I think so," she said. She knew she ought to say more, but doubts were surging through her mind. Maybe the praise was really pity. Maybe she had been really terrible.

"Here's how I think of it. Each pair of characters presents the dancer with a problem. And yours could be this one. How does a sandal-wearing child of love morph into a hardened streetwalker? I mean, they seem miles apart. Free sex as opposed to sex for a price. It's possible she gets into drugs, but drugs alone is a boring trajectory. What does she want? What's her motivating force?"

"I don't know," she said. And then something occurred to her. If the girl was a runaway, things had not been good at home. "Maybe she's angry?"

Ruben smiled. "Yes," he whispered. "I think that's it. That's where desire comes from. It's fury transposed into control. She enjoys having power with men, but when she sees that sex is a business transaction in Times Square, she wants that even more. She knows her youth is the commodity men want and she's going to give it to them, but on her terms, at her price. That's the anger, and with every move, it has to be there in her body."

His skin gleamed and his hair was darkened with sweat. She saw the redness of his eyes, the roughness of his cheeks, and she felt something inside her that washed the doubt away. "Yes, thanks. I can see how that might work."

He patted her arm. "By the way, we haven't talked business. So hang on and let me find my papers." He pulled his satchel over to the chair and extracted a folder. There was a tax form that she had to fill in and sign, and then a contract. She wrote her name without reading it and handed it back.

"Read it," he said.

It laid out the number of rehearsals, the number of performances, and then a weekly salary, which was more money than she thought she'd ever make in her life.

10.

"Yes, that's very nice," Cleo said, "but I'll tell you something. The government's going to take most of it. Better if it was under the table. That's how my jobs were. Under the table plus the opportunity for tips. There's no tips in this. See, that's not good."

Ava explained that this was a different kind of dancing, but Cleo didn't listen.

"There's ravioli. It's on the stove. And if you want more, there's another can." She aimed the remote towards the TV, but before she turned up the sound she said, "You'll like this, by the way. Bring out your plate and we'll watch it together."

"What is it?"

"Oh something, I forget the name. Something with that, oh, what's her name, Shirley MacLaine."

Under the fluorescents, Ava inspected the left-over pasta. What she wanted was the kind of food she made for Mr. Abram, but the only vegetable in the refrigerator was a stalk of celery.

The next day she bought ingredients to make her own dinner. This became a habit. Each night, on the way home from rehearsal she'd stop at a market for vegetables and meat or fish. Sometimes she made extra for Cleo, but most often her mother would have no more than a taste and declare that her stomach was too sensitive for new things.

Before the rehearsals, Ava went down to the laundry room in the basement and on the cement floor, she practiced her moves. She had no clue about anger. How could you be a sexpot with anger? A sexpot was flirtatious. Long looks, slow moves, hip action. Had Cleo been angry? She was certainly angry now. But back then, sequined, stockinged, heeled, she had been in charge. She was young, but when she was on stage she was in control. Nothing could touch her. Same now, on the bus. Nothing could touch her. She was in charge. Maybe that was it, angry people sought control. So what the sexpot did was make her body a weapon. A sword. She flashed it and flung it about because as long as men wanted her she was safe. But how did you put all of that into the moves? She used the washers and dryers as her props. She strutted and draped herself, worked on splits and kicks. She danced for the machines, showing off, pulling away, teasing.

At rehearsal, they spoke about things she'd never considered: intention, phrase, beat, timing. She didn't know how to talk that way, but every night, before she went to sleep, she went down to the laundry room and teased the machines to death, doing the new moves over and over.

Her body was changing. She was building muscle. Her scattered, casual energy was focused now: she practiced until the moves became easy and then, automatically, found herself creating a style for each of her characters. That helped her figure out attitude. Attitude was the style of movement. She gave the runaway a restless, naïve abandon. She was always running, leaping, twirling, tumbling because stillness was the ultimate danger.

The prostitute role required hatred. The five-inch heels she wore helped. She became tall in her mind and the forward, off-balancing thrust of the shoes was torture, one she got used to, but in the beginning, when she was just figuring out how to move in them, they made her feel so robotic it was easy to imagine that her flesh was steel. The iron hooks and pulleys in the rehearsal space suggested the menace of the prostitute's world and sometimes, when they went off to different corners of the room and practiced moves on their own, their immovability helped her in the same way as the washers and dryers. I will make you want me, she thought, and no matter how hard she worked at it, they never showed emotion.

During the first weeks they practiced the male and female sections separately. Later, when Ruben put them together, there were lots of mistakes; sometimes they would inspire him to make a change and that would screw things up for awhile. But the excitement was always there, the challenge of creating something with other people.

Toward the end of the three weeks, they rehearsed with costumes and makeup. Ruben handed her tight red shorts and a black lacey top. He threw a bra on top of the pile. "Hope it fits," he murmured, "Brekka bought it for you."

Brekka and Evelyn changed into their costumes on the floor, in front of the men, everyone standing around in their underwear, but Ava took hers into the little bathroom in the hallway outside.

"Your costumes are your characters," Ruben told them. So whenever they wore them, they had to be in their part. Ava sat on the toilet and became quiet. She pictured Cleo in her bar outfit, hearing the jeers and taunts the women endured. Why was it so easy? Why was all of it so easy when she had never done anything like it before?

"I'd do anything for those tips. And you know what, the music trances you. It makes you do things." How many times had she heard that?

Ernie Abbott, the pimp, sidled up and took her into his arms, pulling her into a steamy dance they invented together, pausing when the piano paused, building when it built, and moving as one. At first, Ava pulled away as though in protest, but she was only teasing, only making him want her more, and when he couldn't stand it in any longer, she closed in with sudden acquiescence and let him overcome her. The piano and horns built to a great screeching moment and the room exploded into hoots and whistles. It embarrassed her. She hadn't known anyone was watching, but the music did what Cleo said it would do, it put her into a trance and she had known every move, every gesture as though this were the dance she had always done.

There were problems with some of the costumes. The jackets and skirts the women wore for the secretary dance were too tight to accommodate their moves. Ava, in ragged bell bottoms, had no issues, but she wanted to show off the ridiculously wide bells of her pants legs and couldn't figure out how. The secretaries pinned the places where their costumes had to be let out. Then a wan, tired looking Evelyn forgot a transition and she and her partner held the others up till they worked it out.

It was late when everyone left the studio. Businesses had long been closed and the streets were deserted. Ava's subway station was ten blocks away and Ruben offered to walk her there. But then he said, "Just stay at my place. There's an extra bed because Jack's away."

Jack was his roommate, Ava knew that from earlier conversations. "If you're sure it's okay." Under her coat she was wearing the prostitute costume though she'd exchanged the heels for street shoes.

"It's fine. It'll be more pleasant for you and we'll get to visit a little. I can even give you clean sheets because I did the laundry today. Will someone be worried if you don't show up?"

"My mother won't even know. She leaves for work so early she won't miss me."

They were the only ones on the narrow, dark street, Ruben in a long black coat, his great strong stride and moving shape, Ava hurrying under the glare of the street lights to keep up.

It was an old tenement building; they climbed up and up, the tight stairway and narrow halls taking them past invisible lives till finally, at the top, they reached the place Ruben called home. He flicked on a light and walked through the living room to dump his coat and satchel on the sofa. Ava did the same, looking all around, thinking, these walls see him all the time, these floorboards hold him. He showed her the rooms, Jack's on the right, his on the other side with a galley-style kitchen and bath at the other end. "It's not elegant, but we like it." As he pulled linen out of the closet she went into the kitchen and called, "Shall I make tea?"

"That would be very nice."

His kitchen was not like Harvey's at all. There weren't many dishes and in the refrigerator, which she opened out of curiosity, there wasn't much food.

He stood at the door, eyes drilling into her. "Darling, you didn't change." And then, pulling her into his arms, he whispered softly, his lips nicking her ear, "You sweet little cocksucker."

She knew what to do and she realized she had always known. She pressed against him and everything she had been feeling for so long poured into her body. "Can I sleep with you in your room, please?" She whispered it. And then she rubbed against him, back and forth, but he pulled away. He went into the bathroom and closed the door. "Ava, take the costume off. On Jack's bed there's some things. Help yourself and when you're changed, call me."

It felt like a slap.

They sat with cups of tea, looking not at each other but at the cracked and stained plaster of the wall in front of the couch. "I can't do it, Ava. We have a professional relationship and I never get involved with people I'm doing a show with."

"Well, you started it. I was just following your lead. You called me that name."

"I did and I'm sorry. It slipped out. The costume works, you know. And all your little moves, they work."

She took a deep, shuddering breath. The outsized, out-of-control feeling had shifted quickly and seamlessly to shame. "After the performance? Could we? When everything's over? Could you, like, just....." She couldn't say exactly what she wanted because it was simply him. She wanted him.

"I'm too old for you, Ava. You must know that. Isn't there someone your own age?"

"Not really. I'm sort of peculiar. Really. I was always separate. Always alone, except there's my mother." Another deep shuddering feeling rose up from her body. "You don't know how it is. Because I think I need a little help."

"I'm not the one, Ava. I'm sorry, I can't be." He scooted next to her and wrapped her in his strong arms. "We're fags, Jack and me, didn't you know that? We're as good as married. I thought you knew. And I'm sorry, I really thought..."

"Then why'd you say it, that word?"

He pulled her even closer, petted her hair, sighed. "I don't know. And it's way too complicated to figure out. And it's late. We both need to get some sleep."

11.

Ernie Abbott's roles were pimp and banker. He was a short, thick, tightly muscled man with a chin of sandy whiskers and a perpetually surprised look that broke into a grin at unexpected moments. He lived in New Jersey and sometimes when she came to rehearsal he was camped out at the doorway waiting for Brekka to arrive with the key.

One day Ava too came early, and maybe on purpose. He patted the concrete next to him and said, "Hey! How's life?'

She knew the expected answer, but the mixture of surprise and wariness on his face prompted her to say, "I didn't realize Ruben was gay."

"You didn't? Yeah, well, I guess I sort of assumed it. I don't think about that stuff much. Each to his own, you know?" He looked up at the grey wintry sky and hunched deeper into his jacket. He laughed. "I'm not. In case you were wondering. I mean, I just thought I would like you to know that."

"I do," Ava said, and then she surprised herself utterly by adding, "and I think you should suggest we have dinner together, but nothing fancy."

"Yeah," he mumbled. "I was kinda thinking that too."

"Since you seem to get here so early and everything. I could come early too."

"Yeah, that'd be great. There's this really good noodle place and it's cheap." He pointed in a vague direction. "But we should meet here first."

"Sure," she said. But she didn't even have to say it. He was assuming the answer would be yes.

"What time?" he asked just as she asked it too. They laughed.

"Hard to dance on a full stomach. So a little bit early?"

"Good plan. Six?"

"Be all digested and ready by eight? Sounds good."

Saigon Palace. Tastes she'd never imagined. Ginger, lime, something sweet. A huge bowl of string-like noodles in red, oily broth. "This is so good. Oops, I shouldn't slurp."

"Go ahead. They slurp." He indicated the other patrons, people she assumed were Vietnamese. They raised their bowls to their mouths and sucked the noodles off chopsticks.

She laughed. "I'm so happy." But she didn't go on because she realized it was private. This place in her life, a man sitting across from her, a performance about to happen, a friend in Ruben and Harvey, and a talent she didn't even know she had. So she said, "I'm so happy to have discovered this place. Thank you."

He lowered his voice. "The other good thing about this place is it's out of the neighborhood. I never go to Giorgio's, do you?"

"Oh, you mean?" She pictured the bar next to the dance factory with its darkened windows. "I've never even been inside."

"The others go there. For drinks sometimes. You've never been invited?"

"No, it frightens me. Too dark."

"It's not bad. You'd be okay."

"Do they drink a lot?"

"Dancers don't drink. No. Ruben almost nothing. Selzer for Ruben."

They laughed.

"But they gossip," he added in a whisper. "They say things about you."

"Like what?" It was preposterous that anyone would find the subject of her interesting.

"And me. I'm sure they talk about me too. We're like . . ." he opened his hands.

Ava leaned towards him and in a conspiratorial tone said, "What are we like?"

"We're different from them. Younger, not as professional. I mean, I've been in five of Ruben's gigs, but yeah, the others have been at it for years. Hard to tell, though. Like with Evelyn."

She nodded agreement, happy to have a secret with somebody. "The way she couldn't get that transition? I didn't see what was so hard about it."

"Right. Pretty lame. If it was me, I'd of been embarrassed." He sat up, crossed his legs, head tilted to the side. Then he leaned over the table and said in a low voice, "There's something I've been meaning to ask you. Our duet, you know. The pimp one? I think what we invented that first time we wore costumes? Remember? It was better than what Ruben choreographed. So much better. Fresh and alive and original. We're good."

She saw a patch of tiny pimples on his chin and a few blond beard whiskers poking up among them. "Really? I love his piece though. Those dips. It's like I'm elastic."

"Yeah, the dips are good, but don't you think…" He looked at her in a surprised way, then leaned in again. "Can I be honest with you?"

"Sure," she said simply.

"What we did was much better and his thing sucks." Then he leaned back in his chair, looking at her, waiting.

She knew what he wanted. And for a moment she was unsure. Ruben was her friend, but Ruben was a faggot. She could not love him all the way. And this man wanted an accomplice. He wanted sex. He was asking right then and there. And he was strong. He dipped her down, brought her back up with the smoothest, most effortless grace. "Oh yes," she cried. "We were so much better. Ruben's thing sucks!"

Her happiness grew. Because now, to her list of accomplishments, she could identify the feeling that had been growing inside her despite the slap, despite the shame. Sex. All she had to do was shift it from Ruben to Ernie. How he looked at her, what he was willing to say to get her on his side. She'd never guessed she had such power.

"Ava, use your tail. You're not using your tail. God gave us the behind to attract a mate. Use it."

Now they were not only in costume but in makeup, too. The transformation was violent. Angry red lips, bruised eyes, scarlet cheeks. Any place her eyes rested got singed. Her face made her so powerful, she had forgotten the switching, impatient backside, the take-me signal, the undulating muscles that called to any hungry man lounging on the street. And when she got it going, and then worked in the face too, the tits, the shoulders, her pimp couldn't contain himself and the music barely held their mad, evil energy.

The runaway with the beautiful fans at the bottom of her pants (she learned to ripple them out with a fast leg toss) was pure respite. Her careless, sweet, goofy moves were a contrast to the robotic secretaries. But the runaway was careless only for a short while. The banker kept walking past her, back and forth, back and forth, trying to restrain the goose step that was irrupting out of his casual moves, until finally it took over and the hippies on the drums beat out a march as he grabbed her arms and threw her in the back of his car.

"That's it!" Ruben cried, waving his hands to stop all action. "It doesn't matter that we don't know what actually happens to her. What we'll see is the birth of anger." But then he corrected himself because he got the message on her face. "You're right Ava, not the birth, the explosion of it because the anger was already there. You've told us that in the ridiculous goofiness of her moves, her total imperviousness and lack of defenses. The anger explodes into a burn and that's when the hooker is born. So let's see it. Now, get yourself out of his car and show us."

She didn't know how. She was a virgin. How could she even imagine? Cocksucker. With a strange man, for money. Cocksucker, cocksucker. She hardened her body, flung it into that deep and relentless hunger: give it to me. Not love, not sex, money. She became that word.

The first run-through on stage, with the whole company, should have been frightening. But Ava had blinders on. Nothing touched her. The lights, the sets, the numbers of people, the flurry of activity in the wings. There was so much happening at once she had to stay focused. So when Justin Beckwith, as Sammo, sang his crazy hippie song and the street people swung and twirled, playing their buckets and car parts, creating their rush-hour cacophony as the executives passed back and forth and the pimp waited in the alley, she couldn't listen. She couldn't be the audience; she had to stay separate and unaware. She had to be in her two different roles and the simultaneous levels of the production were irrelevant. The sounds that she made with her feet, her voice, sometimes backed by their rag-tag orchestra, sometimes alone, owned her.

And because they owned her, they didn't awe her. That is, she was simply the runaway, simply the hooker. And because she couldn't be nameless to herself, she invented Dawn for the runaway and Dawna when she started walking the streets.

Cleopatra offered to come to the opening night, but Ava lied and told her everything was sold out. In truth they had offered her three free tickets. But Cleo didn't protest, as Ava knew she wouldn't. She was a creature of habit. Once she got home from her job she never went out.

The first preview was the monster before her. She got through it by pretending it was only another rehearsal. At the end of the show the audience went crazy and when Ava came forward, the applause turned thunderous. Or maybe it was her imagination. She was still Dawn and Dawna and she didn't become Ava until she was sitting in a bar next to Ruben sipping a glass of rosé.

"What's your pleasure?" he had asked, and she had named the only alcoholic beverage she knew of. "As the lady wishes," he murmured, and ordered the most expensive rosé on the menu.

They hashed out the problems. There had been mistakes in timing, missteps in group numbers. She didn't have anything to contribute because as a dancer, she hadn't been there. A friend of Ruben's, another choreographer, suggested that while the secretaries did their staccato march on the stairways Ava should be even more loopy and fanciful below them and there should be no indication of any sexual power. "Let her moves be more girlish, more innocent. That way, when he throws her into the car we will truly be heartsick."

"That's good, Mike. I like that. She's so young and trippy, yeah, that would work well. Make sense Ava?" Ruben squeezed her shoulder.

"Yes," she answered. And it did make sense. She could feel already how she might swoop and soften, how she might be more exuberant.

The reviews hit the papers soon after opening night. One critic gave the dance numbers equal space with the acting. He called it "a revelation." Another claimed never to have seen words, song, and dance so seamlessly blended. It was "haunting, raw, erotic." The remaining performances were sold out and Ruben said he was in negotiations to move the show to a larger theatre for an extended run.

The dressing room was electric with nerves. Brekka was checking the women's makeup and when she came to Ava's place at the table in front of the lighted mirror, she put on the finishing touches and said, "So you and Ernie, friends, right?" She rubbed her finger in grey eye shadow and held it over Ava's face and gently, tilting her chin into the light, smeared it onto her lid, a feather motion that made Ava hold her breath. "You want some advice or no?"

Ava could feel Evelyn listening. "I don't know," she said.

"Should Brekka shut up?"

"I don't know," she said again. And then, gathering breath she said, "I think I'll follow my own instincts. But thank you."

"Yes sweetheart, that is exactly what you should do." Brekka planted a kiss on her cheek and murmured, "You look so vile it gives me the fright."

Ernie had already told her Brekka was a lesbian and she should watch out.

Ruben was an idiot, Brekka was lonely, Evelyn was incompetent. They gloated over these judgments, even as the show gained more and more notoriety. One night, when she was leaving the theatre, Ernie caught up to her and said, "I'm staying over at my friend's tonight, and he's out of town, and maybe you'd like to come over for a glass of wine?"

She knew what he was asking and although what she really wanted was to get on the subway and be in her own bed forty five minutes later, she said, "Where does he live?" And it was not far and it was too hard to resist the imploring face or her own sense of momentum. At last she would know.

"Do you have condoms?"

"Oh what a girl, what a question!"

"Well, if we're going to have sex, I want to be smart about it."

The friend's apartment was a single room crammed with possessions. The bed was raised above a desk with a ladder going up the side. He offered wine. But she was too tired. "If you really want to know, what I really want is a huge piece of really fine chocolate cake. With homemade buttercream frosting. From an Italian bakery. Can you find such a thing? If I wait for you here?" It was her right, as the virgin, to make such demands. And though he shot her his surprised look, he was already reaching for his jacket and checking his pockets for bills. Once he had left, she was alone with her feelings: her excitement, her fear.

She rummaged in the closet till she found clean sheets for the bed. Curiously, there were candles on every surface, stuck on plates and tin can lids, all in various stages of slump. She arranged them about the room, wondering why one person would want so many going at once. But when she lit them and turned off the lights, the wavering points of yellow were magical. She found cleanser and scrubbed the filth from the bathtub and ran a high bath of very hot water. She set candles around the tub. Then she took off her clothes, sat down in the water, and promptly fell asleep and everything that happened afterwards felt like it was part of a long, watery dream.

The kisses. What she learned was that when a person decided they were going all the way, the kisses deepened. Mouths turned searching, insistent. The tongue, the hands, the stiff, blind horn on the man, eager to butt past all impediments. She had never imagined how artful it was, how slippery. Nor would she have guessed at the way she knew what she didn't know at all. They ate the cake afterwards. It was laced with a liquor that left a dark, bitter taste in her mouth. He put on music from the performance and as Ava, not Dawn, not Dawna, she did her own moves to it, naked.

12.

Now Ava came in later, left earlier. But at least she still came, still cooked, still graced his lonely rooms with the same energy the reviewer had fallen in love with. Only Harvey knew it had nothing to do with the role she played and everything to do with her person.

He wheeled himself to the kitchen door and using the handles Ruben had installed, he hoisted himself to standing and made the tea and the toast, leaving them on the counter for her to bring to the table. He wheeled into the living room and up to his end of the table where there was a pile of that week's magazines and that morning's Sunday Times. The review Ruben had read over the phone to him last night was in Arts and Leisure. He saw the photo, it was Ava of course, and read it himself.

Finally, the door opened. She popped her head into the living room, just long enough to say good morning, aim her happy look in his direction.

"I have something to read to you, so hurry up."

"Be patient, old man. I'm getting there."

Since her, well, what would he call it, her *discovery*, the two separate personalities of the regular Ava and the Thursday Ava were more melded and the new arrogance made him feel more comfortable. Not so fucking unreachable. And *old man*, he loved it. Soon, he would know what derogatory to fashion for her.

She set it all out, sat down. He took a sip of tea, cleared his throat, and said, "There's something that might interest you in the Arts section: "The Charmer Who Dances Her Way Into Our Hearts." He read everything up to the part about her and that he read slowly and in a soft voice: "'Ava Prett, the dancer who plays the California runaway who turns into a Times Square prostitute brings a wild and zany energy to the dance sequences as she loops from sweet-tempered badness to pure malevolence with an originality and focus that is thrilling to watch play out. Her spectacular moments make up for the less than inspired moves of the pimp and financier, danced by Edward Abbott, a performer we have seen before in Ruben Escorella's work.'"

"That's so awful. How could they say that?"

"Awful? Did you hear it?"

"But Ernie! How could they say that? He's the one who makes me look good. I feel so terrible. I mean, what do I know, he's so much more experienced."

"Listen, listen you!" he was shaking like a palsied old man. "Now listen here!" He slapped the table to get her to stop. "Don't denigrate yourself!" Pointing a finger, shouting. "Don't diminish what you do in order to prop him up. Why do women always do that? It's not fair to yourself. Miss Nobody. That's who you are. Nobody! But you're *not* nobody. You breathe, you eat, you shit, you sit at my table and take up room in my apartment. And not only that, you're a surprisingly talented young woman. You take over the stage. And let me tell you, I know what I'm talking about. When you're on the stage, no one in the audience can bear to look anywhere but at you. You've got it! You've got that elusive, mysterious, compelling quality that moves people. So step up to the plate and forget Eddie."

"Ernie," she said. She stood up to carry their dishes into the kitchen. "What do you want for dinner?"

Another typical female move. So he said very plainly, enunciating, "We are having a conversation here and you are not simply going to leave it."

She came back and said, "But we do have to think about dinner," sounding as peremptory as she could, but she was no match for him.

"We do not. We are having a conversation and we are going to finish it. Sit down, Nobody. Tell the old man. Why are you angry?"

"I feel bad for Ernie. And you can't just tell me to forget him."

"Why not? You have something that he doesn't."

"He's my boyfriend."

This he wasn't expecting. "Do you love him?"

"Of course I do, I mean, yes."

"And he's your first?"

She nodded an affirmative.

"And have you talked to him since the review?"

"No, but maybe he hasn't seen it."

"He's seen it."

"He's going to hate me."

146

"If he hates you, drop him. He's no good for you if one little review makes him jealous. Let me tell you something." And without waiting for her to give him the go ahead, he told her about Alice. "I knew the first time I saw her on stage that she had that rare thing. It's what you have. An awareness of the audience. But not only that. It's a desire to do anything for them. Anything. You want them to have a true experience, to carry away something really big and you'll turn yourself inside out to give it to them. Let me tell you, Alice came from the hinterlands. No sophistication. Nothing in her life that I could see gave her this thing she had. She'd learned to sing in her church. Her church! Not Negro gospel, which might explain it, Presbyterian! Milk toast! She was going on nothing! Nothing but feeling and intuition."

As he spoke, he saw her exactly as she had been. Those tanned arms, the long neck, the wrist circled by a silver band. This beautiful creature standing before him. He remembered the time at the Greek restaurant. Summer. A sleeveless dress. In His great wisdom, when God had made the sleeveless dress, yes indeedy, that was the way to ensure that the species would reproduce. His eyes began to tear, the memory was so exquisite. "I had to get out of the way when she became famous. I had to let her surge forward and become who she was meant to be."

"I've never heard her sing," Ava said simply.

"Then let's do it. Let's do it this moment."

He wheeled to the music room. He knew what he wanted to play her. *Evenin'*, it was the opening song on her last album. He shook the record out of the sleeve and gently placed it on the turntable. He didn't play records much anymore, because he wanted to save them, but the sound quality was better on the record than the cassette. He waited, letting the silence crystallize, and then he set the needle in the groove and her voice came into the room. Alice! In all her simplicity and surprise. He looked at Ava and he could see that she felt it too.

The lyrics, they were so plain, but the rhythm was tricky and what the voice did was make it all smooth, all okay. The pain was okay.

Evenin', every night you come and you find me
And you always remind me that my baby's gone.

When it was over, he stopped the record, wiped it off, put it back in

147

the sleeve. Then he wheeled around and saw that she had changed.

Her eyes were glassy too. Her face was loose, softened. "I had no idea. I mean, it's sad, but it's beautiful. It's so beautiful it makes you feel good. It's amazing that she could make me feel that way. I mean, it's like I'm there. In it with her."

"That's what an artist does. They take the horrible things life gives us and they make them bearable by finding the beauty. That's what she gave her audience. That's what they took away."

"I never knew. I never really got it."

She seemed to be in a state. He realized very quickly that he should do nothing but listen. She was struggling to say something and he had to be absolutely focused on her words to help her get them out.

"That I was separate, that I could dance. But it was only because of my mother. We had it. And it made us separate and apart. Or I was separate and apart because her dancing was for sex. I think she was a prostitute. I'm not sure. But I think she was. And that made me separate too. But this dancing is completely different. It's not for something, it's with something. You can't be competitive or on your own."

"Well, that's what music does, it creates a community of people all feeling the same thing. It puts everybody on the same beat."

She placed her hands on her thighs, getting ready to stand up. "Thank you. So. Since you're paying me and everything, shouldn't I make some dinner?"

"No. Just sit. Let's not break the moment."

"Okay." She took her hands off her thighs and looked at him expectantly.

"You can cook something terrific for me tomorrow. Okay? I just feel more like talking today. Is that all right with you?"

"What would you like to talk about?"

She seemed so normal, so forthcoming he had to remember it was Ava. "This theater work is good for you. Gets you out of your shell."

"I sort of feel like I'm on my way. I don't know; I've never felt that before. On my way."

"Towards what?"

She shrugged, hands splayed on her thighs again. "I don't know.

Towards whatever will happen. Towards the next thing."

"Well, what do you see out there? What do you picture for yourself in ten years?"

"Me and Ernie'll have our own apartment and we'll both be dancers. Maybe by then we'll be on Broadway."

She said it without hesitation so he cautioned gently, "You know, often, not always, but often a first love doesn't last very long."

"We'll last, I really think so."

"Well, I'm glad it's that good for you. That's nice to hear."

"How do you see yourself in…."

She was going to say ten years, but he saw that she realized he wouldn't have ten years.

"In the future." The smile, acknowledging it. She wasn't afraid to look at him.

"Dead." He said it with finality. And he could see her fill up with all of the arrogance of the young and healthy, ready to protest.

"No, no, none of that. Dead is what I want. It's the next step. And it's not such a terrible thing. Alice and I, in the later years, when Ruben and Jennifer were gone, we had a little project. We called it Sunset Park. But that's for another day. I'm feeling very tired all of the sudden. So I'll just wheel into my room and you could take some leftovers out for my dinner. And I'll see you tomorrow."

She leaned down and placed a kiss on his temple. He reached for her hand. He held it, pressing his thumb into her palm, sealing what had just happened. It was a moment. Then she went into the kitchen and he wheeled down the hall.

13.

As soon as they were settled in the restaurant she said, "I'm sorry about the review."

"That's okay. He liked you though, didn't he?"

She was prepared for that. So she said, "The only reason I looked good was because of you. It's true, you know."

He shrugged. "I'm really hungry. Let's order."

He wasn't very talkative, but he ate an enormous amount, everything that he ordered plus everything that she had ordered too, none of which she felt like eating. They split the bill, and she left the tip because he said he didn't have any ones.

Out on the sidewalk, she could feel the pressure of all the things he was not saying. It made her want to escape, but she counseled herself to be patient. She would not be like her mother. There would be no "multiples" in her life; she would have one boyfriend. "Why don't we go over there under the trees, sit on that bench?"

"If you want to."

When they sat down she asked, "Are you mad at me for that review? Because you know it's not my fault."

"I'm not mad. And I'm not jealous, so don't be thinking that. But the whole thing sucks. Because I know how this guy operates. He's just trying to get into your pants."

"Who?"

"Erik what's his name, the critic."

"But he doesn't know me. I've never even met him."

"That's exactly my point," Ernie said, turning his pale, pimply face towards her and laying his big, sweaty palm over hers. "You don't know how it works. You ever hear of Maisie Heller? She was this girl a little older than you and she was in this other show I was in and the same thing happened. He gave her this great praise, the show was extended, and she was like this star. And then he arranged to interview her and they became lovers and she dumped him after awhile because he's a real prick. But he took his revenge. He made certain no one would hire her. In the dance world he like calls the shots. Believe me, this guy owns it. He knows everybody and has all this power and he hates me."

"But why? You're so great. Your leads are why I can do all this stuff."

"Because Maisie left him for me. See? I was hosing her. That's how it goes."

"No. Really? This is how he's getting back? Wow, I guess that makes sense. I mean, I didn't think I was that good. Like, how could he mention me and not mention Brekka?"

"Exactly. See, that's how it works." He stopped talking to watch a dog pull his owner from tree to tree. "Look! Who's taking who for that walk?"

"But Ernie, how can you believe in anything then?"

"That's exactly my point. You can't. It's all bullshit. Who's sleeping with who, that's all that's going on, that's only what those reviews are about. You could do like a scientific study and trace it and you'd have all the proof you'd need."

"It just explains everything. It really does."

"Know what I'm thinking? Makes me so pissed I'm really thinking about this and my uncle up in Rochester? He's been after me for the longest time. I'm really thinking I'm through with this dance stuff. Finished. For once and for all. I'm going into business. Up in Rochester. Candles."

"What do you mean? What are you telling me?" She grabbed his arm, hearing his words again and letting their meaning sink in. "Ernie, what are you saying?"

"What I'm telling you, Ava, is that I'm done. Not with you. With dance, with this city. After the last show I'm moving up to Rochester to work for my uncle. Aurora Candles, that's what it's called."

"But what about me?"

"You won't have any problems, believe me. You'll be with Shithead. I'm sure he'll contact you."

"But that's not what I want. I want to be with you. I want you. Don't you know that?"

He smiled. "I guess you'll have to come to Rochester. What's a matter? You'd like upstate." He leaned in and kissed her, and against her cheek, continued talking. "It's really pretty. These great big houses. Loads of shopping centers. How does that sound?"

"Of course," she said, not even knowing where Rochester was. "It's not far, is it? I'll come back to see my mom. What is it, a couple of hours?"

"Hardly anything at all. And it's this small, friendly city. We'd get there just in time for the lilac festival. Hey, maybe my uncle could give you a job too!"

The show was extended, but it didn't move to a larger venue. Most days, before going to the theater, they met for a meal and made plans. Ernie talked to his uncle and there was the possibility of a job with a cousin who needed someone to organize staging for her real estate company. It was a communications job and the only skill necessary was dependability and a reliable car.

"I can't drive," Ava said when he told her.

"Oh, don't worry about that. That's no biggy. We'll work it out. I'll take you wherever you have to go. Or my other cousin. It's all good. And eventually you'll learn to drive. It's easy."

"Okay," she said doubtfully. "but how much does a car cost?"

"No worries, cars are cheap, dirt cheap."

"But my mother doesn't even own a car and she knows how to drive, she drives a bus. It's expensive to own a car."

"Only in New York. It's dirt cheap everywhere else. Cars are how it's done everywhere but here. Trust me." He turned her head towards him and kissed her lips. "It'll all work out and we'll be together. We'll be in a new place and we'll have each other and it will be exciting. I can't wait. I can't wait to get out of this shithole city."

Meanwhile, the sex continued and what she hadn't counted on was the ongoing demands of it. There was something in him that never got satisfied. In a restaurant, on a walk, riding the subway, he'd whisper in her ear, "Let's find a place cause I really want to ball you." Or *fuck you*, or *hose you*, or *drill the living daylights outta you*. The words were different, but the tone was always the same: secret, private, and an assumed privilege.

Was it supposed to make her feel desired? All it gave her was a catalog of hidden locations. She learned the other side of the city, the dark stairways and shadowed corners. Each time, barely concealed by a wall or a tree or trash cans in an alley, they had just enough time to consummate his urge. The danger of it, the possibility of being discovered seemed to add to his pleasure, while it only frightened her. She prayed the back door would not open, or the cyclist would not have to come down the stairs to store his bicycle. She held on, in whatever position she had to maintain for whatever tight little space they'd found, waiting for it to be over.

He kicked the condom into bushes or grass or a gutter, but every time he folded the wrapper, slipped it into his pocket.

So finally: "What is that, a souvenir?"

"I'll tell you something. What you need to do is get on the pill. Then we wouldn't have to do this."

"Rochester," she promised. "I'll go to a clinic."

14.

The bare activities of life, dressing, making breakfast, wheeling to the door to get the paper, filled up the early morning hours until she got there.

"Hello, old man," she called.

"Hello, Nobody," he called back.

"Did you sleep well?"

He could hear her hanging up her jacket, stowing her bag, walking across the foyer. And there she was. She kissed his temple. "Your hands are cold," he said.

"It's chilly, though maybe it'll get warmer later on and we could go for a walk."

"That would be grand."

She brought in the teapot, the two cups, the plate of toast, the dish of marmalade, her glorious self. But she didn't pour. "We'll let it steep."

"Whatever you say," he offered because he was her acolyte.

"I have to tell you something and it's going to be hard."

"Just say it," he recommended, heart thumping.

"I'm moving to Rochester. As soon as the show's over. In two weeks. I'll get there just in time for the lilac festival, which is a really big thing up there. There's this park with the biggest collection of lilac trees and the most varieties of anywhere in the whole world."

"I believe they're considered to be a bush. Interesting. Rochester, New York, whatever for?" He smelled sex.

"Ernie's going to quit dance and get a job with the Aurora Candle company."

"And what will you do?"

"I'm getting this job as a real estate photographer."

He must have looked surprised because she said, "You don't really have to know how to take pictures. They give you a camera and teach you the whole deal in less than an hour."

"Marvelous."

"I thought you would be upset."

"I am. I'm being sarcastic."

"Oh." A pause, but then with enthusiasm, "Is the tea ready, do you think?" She poured some into his cup, and it was dark enough. "I mean, the agency will send someone else. I've already told them and I said, send him someone young and female."

"Thank you, but I won't be needing anyone. I'll be fine on my own. I was fine before, remember?"

"I know you can do everything, but you need to have some company during the day. You're by yourself too much."

"Well, that's the nature of it. I've always been a lonely person and so of course that's what I am now. It's my natural state. I would feel it even if I had a roommate."

"Okay." But her eyes were restive. They drifted about the room and then came back and she said, "Wow, you're taking this better than I thought you would. I was just dreading it."

"Listen, Ava, don't diminish your importance in my life. I have a tight hold on my feelings so I'm not going to whine or complain or cry or get angry. At least not while you're here." He pushed into the table and took a piece of toast and slathered it with marmalade. But when he lifted it to his mouth, he found he couldn't take a bite. He would simply die. That's what he was going to do. As soon as she left for good he would go into the bedroom and lie down and not wake up. (You pathetic old fool! Eat the fucking toast. She has her whole life and all of her loves and happinesses and you are not to make her feel guilty.) He cleared his throat, dabbed his mouth in case there was spittle. Then he dabbed his eyes because lately, they kept tearing for no reason. "Don't forget, I'm living in Sunset Park."

She looked at him blankly. Of course. She was so wrapped up in her own plans she was careless with the things he imparted. And of course she was, it was appropriate.

So he explained again how, when the kids were grown up, he and Alice had a project called Sunset Park. "Life happens in Sunset Park, you see."

"It's somewhere in Brooklyn, isn't it? Near that big cemetery. I went there once."

"Greenwood Cemetery, yes. But I'm not talking about the actual place. It's a metaphor. You know metaphors?"

"Yes, I took honors English and I did pretty okay."

"It was our way of talking about old age and death. And since she's been gone, I've expanded the concept."

"Harvey, sorry, but I have to use the bathroom. I'll be right back. I'm really interested."

While she was gone he came to his senses. Do not talk about it, he instructed. It's private, and it's totally irrelevent for someone her age. And then, all of the sudden, he was so exhausted, he couldn't keep his eyes open. And suddenly he was in motion. Had he died already? Was it an angel wheeling him to paradise? "Where are we going?"

"I'm taking you to bed. For a nap."

"No! I'm awake. And I want to be in the living room to read the paper. Also, we have to cook something. Take me back."

"Your eyes were closed and you were snoring really loud."

"Oh God, that's embarrassing. So, what are we going to make?"

"You have to eat your toast. And then you have to tell me about Sunset Park."

"Well, Sunset Park was the title of Alice's last album which was all blues. She was a great blues singer. A white girl from a little coal mining town in Pennsylvania. Her real name was Wisniewski, but she could sing the blues, as you heard."

"Yes, and I want to hear more."

"Don't humor me."

"I'm not, old man."

"All right, little Miss Nobody. "Slow Dancing in Sunset Park," that's what it was called."

"So what is it?"

"You haven't guessed?

"No, I haven't," she whispered happily, stroking the back of his head.

That brought him to his senses. "Well of course you haven't, you're too young. And I have no business telling you about it."

"That's not fair. You're teasing me."

"No, I'm not, I'm just not going to dump my shit onto your shoulders. And that's why I am going to shut up about it."

She carried the breakfast things into the kitchen and when she came back she fired off a prepared speech. Her whole body was taut with resolve. "What if I want to hear about it? What if I want to have you tell me? Huh, old man? What if I respect you, Harvey, and learn things from you? Okay? So please, if it's not too personal, tell me about Sunset Park."

"Hey, you're good! You're really good. All right. I'll do as you say. It was our philosophy and it's very simple. Each human, as soon as they get squeezed out of the womb, is living in Sunset Park. Death begins the day after we're born and everything we do determines the kind of death we will have. Do you have honest relationships? Do you say the hard things? Do you take the trouble to make sure that what you're telling someone is the truth? Are you courageous enough to do the things in your life you feel passionate about? Even though they might terrify you and cause hardship?

"When the project began, we were living in Scarsdale. Two cars, a lot of driving, a lot of commuting into the city. Once the kids left home, it didn't make sense. We wanted to simplify our lives as we got older. Well, we knew we couldn't live close to Jennifer, she was in Illinois, but Ruben was in the city and we could be close to him. So we put the Scarsdale place on the market and we looked for an apartment that would be a short walk to the park and shopping and subways. We wanted to be high up, have beautiful views. I dropped all of my clients except Alice and we put our energies into two more recordings. But sadly, as it turned out, it was only one. It was a wonderful time. Our lives were focused on each other. We listened to music, she sang, we read out loud and at night we drew a high bath before we went to bed and lowered our decrepit old bodies in it and soaked together. We drank good wine at good meals that I cooked. There wasn't much sex, though there was some, and we were in love. Sunset Park was the last recording she ever made and I think she knew it would be the last. She knew she would go early. Her timetable was different than mine and this whole Sunset Park project had been her idea. She wanted to be ready. But more than that, she wanted to create a life that she could enjoy as long as possible. And she did. She was here and there and out and about until her last week. She was suddenly very tired, very weak, but there was nothing to indicate she needed to go to the hospital. And one night she was gone.

"You, Ava, are in Sunset Park as much as I am. What you decide to do in your life, the decisions you make now, will determine the kind of aging you will have. Will you have said the things you wanted to say? Loved the people you wanted to love? Done the hard things, the things that were important to you, the things you were scared of? It starts now."

15.

Ruben had exciting news. Lincoln Center was offering him a commission to stage three Grimm's fairy tales. He'd run the whole show, choosing the tales, the dancers, the music, and the music would be performed by the Count Basie Orchestra.

All of this was announced by the door, while he was still standing in the hallway. Harvey, who was about to sit down to a dinner of Ava's leftovers, was pleased to have company. "Well, come on in, boy. That's fabulous. Tell me everything. Have you told Jack?"

"I wanted to tell you first. In person. And I brought champagne."

"Very good!" Harvey said and headed for the music room.

"I'll get the glasses!" Ruben called, running in his socks to the cupboard in the living room that was home to the diminishing troubadours and four hand-blown champagne flutes.

"Bring a third! We'll get Alice in on it, too." Before Harvey put the record on the turntable, he flipped the cover to the backside where there was an old, grainy photo. She was blowing kisses to an audience, holding a bouquet of flowers. Newport maybe; he didn't remember. "Our boy," he whispered.

The flutes were a soft rose color. They had bought them on their last trip, and the afternoon sun spilling through the windows backlit their delicate hues. As the song played, they held up their glasses, and when it was over, Harvey made up a toast. "May you continue to create memorable works. May you shine on and on, lighting up our world, expressing our innermost feelings in movement." He wiped his watery eyes and as they clinked their glasses Ruben said, "To my father and mother with all my love and all my thanks for giving me what I needed and putting up with a lot of shit."

"A lot of shit," Harvey echoed. They clinked to that and took turns draining Alice's glass.

"I'm going to ask Ava and Brekka, but I've decided not to use Ernie. He's too big an ego, too hard to work with."

"Oh shit," Harvey said. "They're together, you know. In love. Did you know that?"

Ruben winced. "Jesus, how could she?"

"Never doubt the stupidity of youth or sex."

"Or the power of smooth talking."

"Nevertheless, if I were you, I'd get her to sign on as soon as possible."

"Right, sealed, signed, delivered. I'll talk to her soon."

"If I were you I wouldn't wait."

"But Dad, you're not me."

Ruben's face assumed the old bluntness. He thrust his chin forward just as he used to; his fists were clenched, his shoulders strained. But it wasn't an eleven year old boy who spoke, it was a man with a deep voice. "That's the problem; that's always been the problem, and I'm sick to death of trying to be as good, as organized, as perceptive a person as you." And then he grinned, everything relaxing, and he laughed out loud. "I got you! I got you! I could see you cringe! Oh God, I trained you well. But you trained me too. And I'll grab her soon, but there's a millon details." He corked the bottle and made leaving preparations that Harvey pretended not to mind. "Jack's waiting and he doesn't know yet, so I'm going to take this with me and run.'"

Harvey wheeled after. "Hey, bring Jack by sometime. I haven't seen him in ages."

His hand was on the door, but he turned back to salute his father, his face electrified. Harvey knew exactly how it felt when there was a person at home you absolutely couldn't wait to see. He listened to his boy's footsteps down the hall and turned to face the empty rooms.

Then he went to the toilet, and though it was early and dinner was untouched, he lay down on his bed. Sleep was the only thing he wanted.

16.

"So where is Rochester?"

She could answer because she'd looked at a map. "Top of the state, towards the west, and there's a train to New York. Twice a day."

"What is it? Some dance thing?" Cleopatra held the remote in front of the TV and the terrible screams stopped so abruptly the quiet was miraculous. She swung around in the lounger, set the box of crackers on the coffee table, and took a sip of rosé. "I'm not ready for this. It's too sudden and all right, I understood about the job and the performance because you have to grow up, you have to do something. But there's no going to Rochester. That's where I put my foot down. And why? Why would you go somewhere like that?"

So she explained all over again about Ernie's uncle and the job at the Aurora candle factory and her job with the niece who did real estate.

"Doing what?"

"Photographing furniture arrangements in empty houses that are for sale. It's called staging."

"Since when do you know how to photograph?"

"Since never. But you don't have to know. You learn it."

"Sounds cockeyed to me. And especially since she's never met you and I've never met this boy Ernest. And to tell you the truth, Ernest is one of those names I'd never trust. Like Loyal. You meet a guy named Loyal and you know he's a two-timing son of a bitch. It's too much. It's too much to put me through."

"You could meet him."

Cleo poured more rosé, took a cracker and dunked it in. "I don't want to meet anyone named Ernest. Names say a lot and you got to listen to what they're telling you."

"He's a dancer, Mom, he's really good. He taught me everything."

"Exactly, see, it's just as I thought. No one teaches another person anything at all. You get it through your genes. I was a performer and you are a performer. Like mother, like daughter, you know what I'm saying. There's a good movie. How 'bout you stay home and we watch it together?"

"I have to go. I have to meet Ernie."

Cleo was about to point the remote, but she put it down before clicking. "Listen Ava, I don't want to stick my nose into things that are none of my business, but you and this Ernest. You taking precautions? We never had those talks you're supposed to have. I just figured, I don't know..."

"It's under control. And I have to go."

All of a sudden Cleo collapsed, hand to her bosom, her face wretched. Ava grabbed for her, but no, she was laughing. Full-out. She calmed down enough to say, "That's not any kind of an answer. And if you think it is, then I gave birth to an idiot. Life is never under control. Now... wait a minute." She was chuckling now. "I'll tell you what you're doing. I'll tell you. Just a minute. Oh sweet Jesus!" There were more choking sounds and then she said straight out: "You're leaving me! I'm an old couch and you're putting me out on the curb! You're leaving me, child: that's what's happening here. First the name change, then the job, then this dance thing and I don't know the first thing about any of it. And then, as if that isn't enough, Ernest, but who is Ernest? I just hope you're using precautions and I just hope he's a nice boy. Though I'm warning you he might not be, so go on, get it over with, I want to get back to my movie."

That night, on stage, right in the middle of a series of bends and splits, Dawn looked out and saw a familiar face in the first row and simply went on with the same energy and focus because it didn't matter. She was not Ava. At intermission, after she'd changed into Dawna, she wasn't even tempted to think about it. But after the performance, when she heard a familiar voice in the green room, she paid attention.

"Of course I'm her mother. Keep looking. Cause see now, you're looking and you're knowing that I'm the one bequeathed all that talent. The originator. That's who I am. I used to dance the burlesque. Now I drive. It happens. MTA Bus 79. What happens is the body gets old, it has to, and opportunity disappears."

She must have cornered one of the hippies. Quickly, Ava finished taking off her makeup and opened the door to the room where everyone else was congratulated by visitors who came to see them perform, and Ava, until now, had never met anyone but strangers.

"There she is!" Cleo boomed, walking forward to take Ava into her arms. "Back then, I was this small, this limber."

Who was she talking to?

It was Brekka who held out her hand now saying, "Mrs. Prett, I'm so pleased to meet you. And as I'm sure you know, you have a wonderfully talented daughter. She's been a pleasure to work with and a real surprise."

"That's good," Cleo murmured. "Real good. This like a professional situation. An art piece. This is not what I did. So I'm glad for her. Glad for her to be working with a smart and talented lady like yourself."

"Let me introduce you to Ruben," Ava offered, steering her mother away so Brekka could escape. She moved her over to the crowd courting the choreographer.

"Very upscale," Cleo murmured. She winked. "No throw-up, no beer smell. Very upscale. No cigarettes. Not for the lechers. This for the educated. But it's not one of those things like you hear about, called happenings. I got it. It's very organized, very nice."

"I tried to tell you."

"You did, you did. And I had to see it to believe you. And it was good. Even though they gave me the brush-off at the office. But I says, over and over, I'm her mom, go ahead, bring her out and ask her, 'cause I want the front row and I want it for free." When Ruben turned to them, she put her hand out and pumped Ruben's up and down. "That's a real fine show, real fine. I enjoyed it."

Ava saw Ruben's shock as he took in the pink, the big breathing pink intensity.

"Yes, good to meet you, and you are?"

Quickly: "This is my mother," as Cleo boomed, "My name's Cleopatra! Mind if I give you a hug? You're such a fine gentleman and a good human being to treat Ava the way you do and give her this chance to make it big."

"No, Mrs. Prett, I should be thanking you because I'm lucky to have the chance to work with her."

"Excuse me. No missus in this situation. Miss all the way."

"Yes, of course."

"I was a dancer once myself. Hard to believe, but that's where she got it. Here." She put a hand to her bosom as though she were about to say the Pledge of Allegiance. "It all comes from here. Like mother, like

163

daughter, you know."

"I'm so pleased. Ava has been such a pleasure . . ." Ruben held out a hand to initiate their parting as new people came in line behind them.

"The pleasure's all mine to make this acquaintance, and Mr. Ruben, if you ever need a large woman. . . ."

He colored and she said, "What I'm talking about is your performance. Can I give you my number? Cause Ava, she's moving to Rochester."

But Ruben, an expert in managing crowds, had already moved to the next group of well-wishers.

During her last week in New York, all of the ordinary comings and goings had a patina of regret. The subway speeding under the sidewalks: she had never appreciated the vastness of the underground network. But Rochester would have subways too. The vistas of long streets, the mixture of old and new buildings. But all cities had that. Even the sidewalks filled with people, but that, too, you would find in any city. The long dark hallway to the dressing room, the notices on the bulletin board, the smell of makeup, the nervousness before the show. She would miss Brekka. She wanted to thank her and say goodbye, but Ernie had made her promise not to tell anyone because they would get on his case about dragging her away. She corrected him: "You're not dragging me. I'm going of my own choice." She was choosing who to love, making the hard choices, going with the things she was scared of so that one day they could be like Alice and Harvey.

But the curtain call of the last performance was the most difficult. Everyone was crying. And when the velvet finally came down and the house lights went up, she hugged them all. She didn't want to let them go; she wanted to take them with her. All she had to do was look at Ruben and she would start to weep. She could tell Harvey hadn't told him. That pleased her. He wasn't gossiping behind her back, he was trusting her to tell Ruben in her own way. And she'd do it soon. But from Rochester, a thank you letter.

When they were with the troupe, they stayed apart. Ernie didn't want anyone to know they were together. And no one did know, although Brekka of course suspected. There was a photographer in the lounge, arranging people in different poses and combinations for pictures. Ruben said he would send everyone copies. They turned their costumes in, and that too, was a powerful moment. But it was only a pair of heels, blue jeans, red shorts, empty containers.

Ava found a suitcase at the top of Cleo's closet. It was well-used, battered really, but everything she wanted fit into it. The sides bulged, threatening the zipper, but she got it closed. She pushed it under the turnstile at the subway and lugged it through Grand Central and once they were on the train, Ernie hoisted it into the luggage rack over their seat. She watched him with amazement, thinking to herself: this is the person I love. Other people came on, squeezed past with bundles and bags. Ernie, who had checked two enormous suitcases into baggage, worried they hadn't made it on. He left to find a porter.

She watched him brush past the people going in the opposite direction. When he had to stop for an obstruction, she read impatience in the set of his shoulders. A woman with too many bags was trying to situate her child. "Sorry," she said, turning to him apologetically. He didn't answer. What an asshole, he was thinking; she could read it from the way he stood.

The doors closed, the train moved out of the station. She had a moment of worry, but the familiar vistas of her city were sliding past, and she needed to pay attention. And then, all was well because he came back, carrying snacks and beer. He was jovial. The smell of food sickened her, yet all she said was "no thank you" when he offered sips and bites. The Hudson, next to them, was flat and gray, unmoving. She knew it had secrets: deep currents and ancient fish swimming through the muck and trash at the bottom.

When the train pulled into Rochester, it was an hour behind schedule. "It's always late," Ernie told her. Uncle David was in a bad mood. He shook hands with Ava, but then moved off to give his full attention to the luggage. On the drive to the place they were going to live, he and Ernie talked about someone in the family named Doug who had dropped out of college. A brother, cousin? She didn't care. They went on one highway after another, the roads huge and smooth, all the cars following their headlights through the dark and featureless landscape. The big car turned at a sign for 2000 Mendon Road, Lilac Estates. She remembered it because she was thinking that one day, Mendon Road would be a place she'd understand and maybe even love. They purred past houses as large as ocean liners, their facades lit as though for a party. The driveway swooshed them into a garage and her door popped open. "Everyone's waiting," Uncle David said, "so don't be long. Go ahead, the apartment isn't locked."

They carried their suitcases up the outside stairway and walked into a thickly carpeted room. Ernie shut the door and promptly took her into his arms. "Far out," he exclaimed, and then, under his breath, "far fucking out!" He kissed her, pulled her pants down, maneuvered himself inside. "Just a quickie," he grinned.

Only on television did a family occupy such an enormous space, but television must be accurate because there it was, and hand in hand, she and Ernie were entering. Dinner was waiting in a big, expensive-looking room with a sunken seating area around a fireplace. The table was piled with things to eat, but the relatives, all of them with hairdos, makeup, and aggressive perfumes, even the men, stood around the table holding drinks. The niece who was going to give Ava the job introduced herself with a handshake. She didn't look healthy. Her skin was slicked with perspiration and the mound of hair framing her face was as solid and unmoving as a helmet.

"Nice to meet you. Morrie said you took the train up. So I have to ask: where's the car? That's the one thing I'm concerned about, a reliable car. You know what I mean? I mean, I am doing you a favor. Everyone said, 'Oh Debbie, do this favor. Ernie's in love and the girl needs a job.' So okay, I'm happy to accommodate. We'll give it a try." She shifted a plank of hair off her forehead and looked everywhere but at Ava. "And as I told him, the photography I can teach you, but it's going to be go here in the morning, there in the afternoon, somewhere else the next day and back and forth to the office. The highways are easy, you'll learn them quick. Do not worry about that. But it's going to be all week long, starting in two days, tons of places. And there's been lots of competition for this job, let me tell you. I turned away a qualified applicant just yesterday. I've turned away many qualified applicants so count yourself very, very lucky. You don't know how lucky you are." Her mouth hung open, her big teeth lined up like soldiers.

"I don't have a car, but I'm happy to take the subway."

She started to laugh, her eyes sweeping Ava's face, trying to convince herself it was a joke. "Oh God, you're kidding, right?"

"Or the bus," Ava added, just to show how flexible she was.

"I hope to God you're kidding. Dora! Dora, get this! Ava is happy to take the subway to the houses. For the shoots! Oh shit, she cracks me up. Or the bus! She's happy to do that too. She's happy to wait with the black people for the bus that never comes. Oh God, I'm dying here, I'm dying. Ernie!" The soldiers were standing at attention. She turned her back to Ava and addressed Ernie who was standing at the table, hunched over a plate of food.

"What? What?"

"You didn't tell me your girlfriend was a comedian." Then she aimed her eyes at Ava. "Seriously, the one thing I said to him: She has to have a car, a reliable car."

"But I can't drive."

"Oh God, now I'm pissed. Ernie didn't tell you? There's no subway in Rochester. There's hardly any buses. And these houses. They're not in the ghetto, sweetheart. These houses are million dollar estates and," as though Ava spoke a different language, she enunciated clearly, "you-have-to-drive-to-them. Give me a break." Throwing her hands up, she left Ava and went to the table. "Give me a fucking break. Ernie? Who is she? What planet does she live on?"

That night, in the garage apartment, as he nuzzled her neck he said, "Earlier? It was just a prelude." Now it was for real, their honeymoon. Or almost. Wasn't it? He really wanted to ball.

"I can't," she mumbled.

"Oh come on, Debbie was kidding. Don't be offended. It'll work out. She'll give you the job and the car thing will happen. It's all good. And look at this fabulous place we have for free. It's like a hotel," he said reverently, body turned to admire the neutral walls, the anonymous furniture, inviting her to admire it too. "Trust me, this is a top-of-the-line mattress." He pulled her down. "Feel how firm."

If she protested, she would start to cry and there would be no stopping of it, ever. So she held herself as still as a board and he got excited without any help from her and bucked and thrashed as he always did. When it was over and he had fallen asleep, she slipped off the expensive mattress and went to the bathroom to clean herself. Then she tiptoed into the living room. Her suitcase was still in the middle of the wall to wall carpeting, unpacked. On the phone in the kitchen she dialed information and when the operator came on, she asked for the number for the train. One was leaving for New York at 5:00 a.m. She got the number for a taxi. Cleopatra had given her two twenty-dollar bills; Harvey had given her two fifties. "Just in case you change your mind," he said, closing them into her hand. Now she pulled them out of her pocket and felt how worn and smooth they were, how indestructible. It was two in the morning and though the cab wouldn't come for another hour, she needed to leave.

She put on her jacket and softly drew the door closed. Outside, everything was hushed. The trees and grass were breathing, fogging the chilly air. She lifted her suitcase, but it was too heavy, so she slid it from step to step, trying not to make any noise. There was a light on at the back of the house, but she skirted it, walking through the plantings and then all the way to the end of the lane, past the other dark residences. At the sign for Lilac Estates she set her suitcase in the grass and used it as a bench. The zipper popped, she heard it. She could hear everything, her heart, her breath. It would be a long wait and there was nothing to see in the sky, no stars, not even a moon, because it was cloudy. But somewhere close there was the companionable sound of water gurgling in a stream and later, when headlights came towards her, then slowed down and stopped, a single bird had started to sing.

The van had a sign on the door, Lilac Transportation. A man leaned out the window and said, "You the one for the Amtrak?"

He saw the problem with her suitcase and lifted it into his arms like a child, set it into the back, and slid the door open. But before he would let her get in he said, "Cost you fifty, up front."

She gave him the money, and as the car sped through the suburbs she sat very still. Her various selves crowded her being, but within the commotion she could feel something singular take hold, something wavering that she wanted to concentrate on.

It lasted all that long day, as she retraced her steps backwards across the top of the state and then down along the Hudson to New York. She focused on that something in the center of her chest; it was entirely her own, and it was gaining in strength.

Acknowledgements

I am grateful to the editors of the literary quarterlies where some of these stories were published in slightly different form: "Mischief" in *The Common;* "Leaving the Meadows" in *The Northwest Quarterly;* and "Mocked And Invaded," "Arrogance," "Tertium Quid" in *The New England Review.*

"American Pictures" and the idea of a traveller who agrees to all proposals is borrowed from a 1985 book by a Danish wanderer named Jacob Holdt who published his experiences in a book of that title. I am grateful to Ann Hamilton for permission to use her photograph on the front cover. Of the several books written about the great choreographer Bob Fosse, *Razzle Dazzle: The Life and Work of Bob Fosse* by Kevin Boyd Grubb, as well as Fosse's dance routines, many of them collected on YouTube, were enormously helpful to my understanding of the performance world in the nineteen seventies. Thank you to Cody Prince and Susan Bain-Lucey for generous help with my questions about massage and public school governance.

Though a work of fiction begins in the sealed environment of the author's imagination, it collects light and air as it moves towards publication. This happens with the help of outside readers to whom I am deeply grateful: Liam Callanan, Greg Pierce, and Nathan Poole. Martha Rhodes' editorial vision was crucial to the realization of these stories and the finished book is the inspired work of Ryan Murphy, Clarissa Long, and Mari Coates at Four Way Books.

Big thanks to Graham Marks, sweetheart and reader extraordinaire.

Megan Staffel's stories have been published in *The New England Review*, *Ploughshares, Northwest Review, Seattle Review,* and other journals, and collected in *Lessons in Another Language* (Four Way Books, 2010). She is the author of the novels, *The Notebook of Lost Things* (Soho Press) and *She Wanted Something Else* (Northpoint Press) and a first collection of stories, *A Length of Wire And Other Stories* (Pym Randall Press). She has published essays on craft in *A Kite in the Wind: Fiction Writers on their Craft* edited by Andrea Barrett and Peter Turchi; *Letters to A Fiction Writer,* edited by Fred Busch; and Cerise Press, Spring, 2013. She divides her time between Brooklyn, New York and western New York State and teaches in the MFA Program for Writers at Warren Wilson College.

Publication of this book was made possible by grants and donations. We are also grateful to those individuals who participated in our 2015 Build a Book Program. They are:

Jan Bender-Zanoni, Betsy Bonner, Deirdre Brill, Carla & Stephen Carlson, Liza Charlesworth, Catherine Degraw & Michael Connor, Greg Egan, Martha Webster & Robert Fuentes, Anthony Guetti, Hermann Hesse, Deming Holleran, Joy Jones, Katie Childs & Josh Kalscheur, Michelle King, David Lee, Howard Levy, Jillian Lewis, Juliana Lewis, Owen Lewis, Alice St. Claire Long & David Long, Catherine McArthur, Nathan McClain, Carolyn Murdoch, Tracey Orick, Kathleen Ossip, Eileen Pollack, Barbara Preminger, Vinode Ramgopal, Roni Schotter, Soraya Shalforoosh, Marjorie & Lew Tesser, David Tze, Abby Wender, and Leah Nanako Winkler.